D1023903

I searched her eyes, trying to read her thoughts. She wasn't meeting my gaze; she was staring at my mouth. "So, if you kissed me right now, it wouldn't feel the same way, right?" Her eyes fluttered and met mine.

My heart flip-flopped. My mind was racing, I didn't trust what I was hearing. She's asking me to kiss her, right? A rushing sound flooded my ears, and I had to remind myself to breathe. I searched her face, just inches away, for an answer. Her green eyes, made bright from the recent tears, were clear and completely focused on mine. My eyes wandered over her high cheekbones, down to her small pointed chin, then dropped to her long neck, and the pulse that was beating at the hollow of her throat. Back to her eyes. Still watching me. Waiting. Not backing down. Beckoning. Her lips. I fashioned myself a thief as I imagined leaning in and stealing a kiss from that mouth. Could she know what she was asking?

Visit

Bella Books

at

BellaBooks.com

or call our toll-free number
1-800-729-4992

Never Say Never

BY
LINDA HILL

Bella
BOOKS

2004

Copyright© 1996 by Linda Hill

Bella Books, Inc.
P.O. Box 10543
Tallahassee, FL 32302

All rights reserved. No part of this book may be reproduced or transmitted in any form or by any means, electronic or mechanical, including photocopying, without permission in writing from the publisher.

First published 1996 by Naiad Press

Printed in the United States of America on acid-free paper
First Edition

Editor: Lisa Epson
Cover designer: Bonnie Liss (Phoenix Graphics)

ISBN 1-931513-67-8

For Debra

Acknowledgments

Special thanks to Barbara Grier for giving me this opportunity; and to Lisa Epson for her illuminating edits.

My love and gratitude to Judy, Barb, Annie, Mary, Ellen, Joyce, and Cheryl.
You have each made me a fortunate woman, indeed.

A big thanks to Mary and Rita, for that last quick read.

Finally, my thanks to Kate and the girls.
When counting my blessings, I always start with you.

Chapter 1

At that moment, the only thing I knew, the only thing I wanted, was for Nancy to get off of me. She was pressing her full weight onto mine and rubbing herself frantically against my leg. No kisses. No gentle endearments. Just groaning.

I couldn't move. I was so angry, so frustrated. *I can't do this anymore.*

"Nancy. Stop," I said quietly. But she continued her feverish grunting.

"Nancy! Stop it!" This time I was yelling as my hands found her shoulders and I pushed her away.

Her body grew rigid before rolling off of me. *Freedom.*

"What in the hell is wrong with you?" she exploded. Jumping from the bed, she began prowling the room. "I am so sick of this shit," she snarled.

I looked away, pushing my head back into the pillow so that I looked up through the darkness toward the ceiling. I was so tired. Exhausted. Fatigued. How many times had we had this conversation? How many times would we have it again?

I took a deep breath to steady myself. My voice, when I spoke, was emotionless.

"I told you that I didn't want to . . ."

"You *never* want to," she spat.

I checked my own rage, knowing that on this point at least, she was right. I no longer wanted her to touch me.

"And I suppose you think that starting a fight in front of my best friend and her lover tonight would somehow make me want to?"

"I don't give a damn what they think." She was leaning over me now, her posture threatening.

"Well I *do* give a damn," I said evenly. "And maybe coming home and fucking is your way of solving our problem, but it's not mine."

"And how do you suggest we solve it?" she sneered.

I sighed deeply, knowing I would never win this battle. I had to leave. I calmly pushed the blankets back and swung around until my feet touched the floor.

"By getting out."

She was temporarily dumbfounded as I padded

2

over to the bureau and pulled out a pair of jeans. I stepped into them and tucked in my T-shirt.

"Oh, that's good, Les. Just run away. That'll solve everything." She tried to goad me, but my mind was made up. I slipped into a pair of sneakers, picked up my keys, and headed for the door, my mind blocking out the steady stream of insults that she hurled.

The next-door neighbor's dog began barking incessantly as I made my escape.

"Shut that fucking dog up!" were the last words I heard as I slid into my car and turned the ignition. At least I was safe now.

I drove the twenty miles to Boston, seeking refuge with my best friend, Susan. She didn't look at all surprised to see me. It wasn't until the next morning, behind the firmly closed door to my office, that I began wondering how my life had ever gotten to this point. When had I lost control?

"The day you met Nancy," I muttered aloud. I'd met her just over two years ago at the annual Gay Pride March in June. She'd been intriguing, exciting, and sophisticated. I wanted her, and she was all that I thought about for six months.

Even though I knew it would never work, I moved in with her and the romance lasted exactly two months. The next year and a half was absolute misery as I slowly lost all perspective of who I was and what I wanted. From the very first day, I knew that I had made a mistake and that I had to find a way out. Yet I stayed, hopelessly believing that eventually I could make her happy, even though I knew it would never happen.

But at least now I had taken that first step. A touch of relief passed over me as I sipped my coffee.

I knew the situation would get worse before it got better, but at least I'd made the break. I wasn't about to turn back now. With that resolve uppermost in my mind, I finished the coffee quickly and answered my boss's summons to his office.

An hour later I emerged from Dennis's office with a barely suppressed grin on my face. The news couldn't have been better. He had offered me a project that would require long hours and more travel than not. It was the perfect opportunity to help get me out of my predicament with Nancy, and I accepted immediately.

I worked for a company that dealt primarily with computer software. It was a young, upstart organization that was turning a hefty profit and always looking for ways to make more. The project that I was suddenly responsible for was to search for an existing financial software package that was solid and well written, but whose sales were floundering due to poor marketing. My company wanted to purchase the software, repackage it, and then market and sell it under our name.

The project was to begin immediately, and I had to work fast to select a team of technical people who would accompany me in my travels. A representative from the marketing group had already been selected to join us. She would be looking at the marketability of the software we would be reviewing. I must admit that I was rather pleased when I heard who would be joining me. I had always been thoroughly impressed by Sara Stevens's professional abilities, and

I looked forward to the opportunity to work with her more closely.

Something very different about Sara made her stand out from the rest of the straight women that I worked with. It had a lot to do with the corporate environment that I worked in. Since my field was data processing, I dealt mostly with men. The women whom I had occasion to work with were usually all very similar. They wore perfect clothes, perfect makeup, and perfect smiles and were perfectly superficial. I was always aware of just how different I was from these women. As a result, I tended to avoid them.

But Sara seemed different. She was incredibly attractive. She had dark brown, wavy hair that fell just below her shoulders. Her eyes were bright green; her skin dark and smooth. Her most appealing physical feature, though, was her mouth. Full lips, blinding white teeth, and a stunning smile. As I got to know her better, I discovered a nervous habit she had of tucking in her bottom lip, letting it go, and then quickly sliding her tongue across first the top then bottom lip before slipping it back inside her mouth. I grew awfully fond of that nervous habit and often caught myself watching for it.

Physical attributes aside, it was her manner, her personality, that I was drawn to. She was sincere and honest. She was also incredibly bright and self-confident, and I had tremendous respect for her opinion and her abilities.

* * * * *

I left work two hours early that day, guiltily sneaking into the apartment that I shared with Nancy and praying that I'd avoid her completely. I tossed most of my clothes into several suitcases and was back in my car within twenty minutes. With a sigh of relief, I headed for the expressway and Susan's rambling Victorian condo just outside of Boston.

Susan Richards had given me her shoulder more often than not during the past few months. She was the first woman who had befriended me since I moved to Boston some five years before. My relationship with her had been as tumultuous, as sweet, and as constant as any I had ever known. She was slightly shorter than I, with dark, nearly black straight hair that she kept rather short. I loved the crispness of it, the way it fell just perfectly over her brow.

When we first met, Susan made it her business to make me feel welcome and introduce me to the city. Initially, I resisted the way she took me under her wing, not trusting her motives. So while part of me was thankful and flattered that she had taken such an interest in me, the wary part of me fought her attempts to get close to me at every turn.

But Susan was persistent in a patient and gentle sort of way. She understood me long before I understood or appreciated her enough. We used to spend tremendous energy having lengthy, heated debates on any topic. It was as though we agreed to disagree on nearly everything. It was expected. Throughout our friendship, she had lovers, I had lovers, she moved, I moved. But the friendship stayed. And grew. I'm not sure when we stopped

6

arguing. I only know that the debates turned to discussions. Discussions gave way to confessions and feelings. We were there for each other. She knew me better than anyone else had ever even tried.

Susan was the only one who allowed me to show her each side of me without being astonished or put off that I could be sweet as an angel one moment and talk trash with the best of them the next. We loved to talk trash with each other. We had great fun at it. And the fact that we knew we were misbehaving somehow made it that much more fun.

Now I was turning to Susan yet again, and of course she was there. When I had shown up on her doorstep the night before, she suggested that I move into her condo.

"You can stay as long as you like."

"What about rent?" I asked.

She grinned wickedly, "I'm sure we can come up with a payment plan." Wink, wink.

"What about Pam?" Pam was Susan's lover. They didn't live together, but they had been lovers for over two years.

Susan shrugged. "She'll get used to it. Besides, the place is big enough for all of us." So for what wasn't the first time, I let her take care of me. I only hoped that some day I could make it up to her.

One week later, the project was in full swing. For that first month, I was on a whirlwind tour of the United States. We traveled as a team of four, shuffling from city to city, airport to airport, one company to another. Sales pitch after sales pitch, we felt like captives forced to smile, be polite, shake hands, and absorb as much information as possible each day.

I had agonized over the selection of the other two team members, eventually settling on two very different men. After that first month, I wasn't altogether happy with my choices.

Frank Bennett was a shy, older gentleman and a real sweetheart. I couldn't help the fondness that I felt for him. In general he was a quiet man, commenting only when asked, trying hard not to show that he was uncomfortable.

I wasn't nearly so fond of the other man in our troupe. Kenny Johnson was young, blond and, I suppose, gorgeous. Women gushed all over him. A walking ego, he knew everything there was to know about computers and made sure everyone knew it. I did my best to maintain my professionalism and steer clear of him as much as possible. I didn't like him much, but I needed him. Which was, more often than not, the way it always was in the corporate world.

The good news was that Sara and I had gravitated together almost instantly. We turned each trip into a special event, working hard, but always managing to have fun along the way. She hated the sales games as much as I did, adored Frank as much as I did, and wasn't the least bit impressed by anything that Kenny said or did.

I had never been wild about traveling, and the project was truly testing my mettle. But no matter how bad it got, all I had to do was think about how bad it would have been if I had still been living with Nancy, fighting night after night. I hadn't really dealt with our splitting up yet. Instead, I pushed her from my mind by telling myself that I would deal with it when I returned to Boston.

Two months went by before I heard from Nancy in the form of a letter, asking me to remove the rest of my things from her apartment before she returned from vacation.

It didn't take long for Susan and me to finish the job, and she was kind enough to stay at my side throughout the weekend. I didn't unpack many of my things since I didn't really expect to be staying at her place for long. I figured that I would store my things at Susan's until the project was over and then find a place of my own.

By early Sunday I was completely moved in and situated. Susan had purchased a futon for the spare bedroom so that I wouldn't have to sleep on the couch when I was in town. "Now don't you get any ideas about bringing any women up here," Susan teased. "I figure that giving you a narrow bed is the only way to keep you out of trouble."

"There goes my social life," I told her with a weak smile. I sat down on the bed and looked up at her, my eyes brimming with unexpected tears. "I screwed up again," I sniffed.

She plopped down beside me, throwing an arm around my shoulders as she did. "No you didn't. The only mistake you made was waiting so long to get out."

"I can't believe I stayed there so long."

She waved a hand. "I knew you'd get around to leaving sooner or later. I'm just glad you finally got out. Besides, you're looking at this all wrong. This is a great opportunity for you. Just think of all the women out there that you can meet."

"Uh-huh." I was pouting, refusing to be cheered up. "Where? In all those airport lounges?"

"Yuck," she grimaced. "Seriously, you should take advantage of all this traveling. Get yourself a gay travel guide and hit some bars. Meet some women."

"I can't just walk into some gay bar. You never know what they're going to be like. And I can't just go up and talk to a woman."

"Please. You talk to women every day. Besides, they'll be falling all over themselves to talk to *you*."

That made me laugh. I always considered myself pretty average looking. On the shorter side with brown hair, cut short so as not to curl too much. Blue eyes. Average build. Not overweight but not exactly skinny either. Average. But Susan always managed to make me feel like a real knockout.

"Okay," I sniffed. "Maybe I'll give it a try."

"Good for you!" She clapped me on the back and was thoughtful. "Hey, what about that woman you started working with? What's her name?"

"Sara?" I was aghast.

"Yeah. What do you think?" Again she grinned wickedly.

"I think you're crazy."

"Why?" she asked with mock innocence. "You keep telling me how hot she is."

I blushed. Had I really told her that? More than once? "Susan," I turned to look at her squarely. "Sara is very straight. Rule number one," I quoted, "never get involved with a straight woman."

"Who said anything about getting involved?" she laughed. "I'm just talking about having a little fun."

I shook my head and laughed in spite of myself. Susan was outrageous.

"Does she know you're a lesbian?"

Again I was appalled. I shook my head vehemently. "Absolutely not. She thinks I have a boyfriend."

"Oh, Leslie, that's disgusting. Why does she think that?"

Now I was growing uncomfortable. "Oh, come on, you know why. Because I let her think so. Because it's easier just to let people think I'm straight." This was a conversation that we, and many of our friends, often had in the past. We had all agreed and disagreed on many levels. There were a few who insisted that we should all be out in the open. That politically it was necessary for us to show that we existed. But the majority of us were only out in various degrees. Some more than others. Some none at all. While we hated it, we admitted that it was sometimes easier to avoid the truth.

"Yeah. I know what you mean. As liberated as I like to think I am, nobody I work with knows I'm gay," she admitted. She was quiet for a while, rubbing my back.

"So why don't you just tell her?"

"Now that sounds like fun!" I laughed. "I tell her I'm a dyke. She flips out and never talks to me again." I laughed at Susan sarcastically. "You really know how to have a good time."

"You never know," she replied in a singsong voice, her eyes twinkling mischievously. "She might just think you're hot too. Why settle for the fantasy when you can have the real thing?"

"You're such a pig." I pushed her away playfully, annoyed. Not by her suggestiveness, I was amused by that. I was more annoyed with the way she always managed to see right through me. "Besides. Who says I fantasize about her?"

She shrugged. "You don't have to tell me. I know you," she said simply.

I was growing more annoyed and wanted the conversation to end fast. "Bad idea, Susan. I can assure you that's not going to happen."

"Not this week, maybe." She smirked at me and, anticipating my growl, smoothly changed the subject.

Chapter 2

I was late arriving at the airport the next morning. Everyone had already boarded, so I made my way down the aisle alone. My three partners were seated together near the front of the plane. Sara, flanked on either side by the two larger men, gave me a meaningful stare when they greeted me. I could almost read her look. *Thanks a lot for stranding me alone with these guys*, it said.

I shrugged an apology and threaded my way back a few rows, almost thankful to be sitting alone. I settled into a window seat and tried to read up on the company we would be visiting, but I lost interest immediately. I was feeling unreasonably emotional, chastising myself for feeling so suddenly lost and woebegone.

The flight attendant came and went, bestowing a bagel and coffee on her way. As I munched quietly and stared out the window at the clouds below, I felt an elbow press into mine and tried hard not to pull away. With an inward groan, I prayed that Kenny hadn't decided to chat.

"Hey, I thought for a while there that I was going to get stuck alone with those guys." Sara's face was inches from my own.

I mumbled an apology, not quite meeting her eyes. Those lips were frowning.

"You don't look so hot."

"Why, thank you. Good morning to you, too," I snapped, feeling bitchy.

"Ouch." She stared at me until I met her eyes. "Uh-huh," she nodded. "You've been crying," she stated.

Was it that obvious? Were my eyes swollen? I looked at her, feeling suddenly vulnerable, and bit my lip.

"Leslie, what's wrong?" She sounded so sincere that it made me feel worse. I didn't want to talk to this woman. I didn't want to be vulnerable with this woman. I foolishly just wanted her to stop being nice to me.

I tried to wave her off, but she wouldn't give up.

"Talk to me. What happened?" She was tugging at me.

"Nothing, really." I fought hard not to let the

tears well up again. "I, uh, I had to move out over the weekend."

"You and your boyfriend broke up?" She looked genuinely distressed as I scrambled for a reply.

"Something like that," I mumbled.

"Oh, Leslie, I'm so sorry." She squeezed my upper arm gently. "I thought you lived with a guy, but I wasn't sure. You never really talked about him."

"No, well, you know —" I stuttered, trying to think of something to say. "We haven't really been getting along. You know?"

"You poor thing. Why didn't you tell me about him?" she admonished. "What's his name?"

I looked at her, feeling incredibly nervous and at the same time dangerously close to giggles. It was absurd. She was staring at me, waiting for a reply. *What was the question?*

"What?"

"What's his name?"

Quickly the names flew through my mind. *Nancy . . . Hmm . . . Nick, Ned, Neal, Noel . . .* I scrambled mentally, but nothing sounded right. I threw up my hands. "What difference does it make now?" I asked, hoping she wouldn't press any further. "It's over."

"Good for you!" She fell for it, and I was relieved. "And when you're ready to meet new people, just let me know. I know a couple of guys that you'd really like." She was getting excited, leaning forward and closer to me. "We could double date."

"Double date?" I nearly choked on what was left of my coffee.

"Sure. You probably aren't ready to meet anyone

now. But I've been going out with this guy, James, and I would love it if we hooked you up with one of his friends so that we could all go out together. Wouldn't that be great?"

"Great. Sure." I couldn't believe what I was hearing, or what I was getting myself into. My anxiety level was rising. "But you know it's probably going to be a while before I start going out again."

"That's okay." She held up a hand for emphasis. "I won't push. I'll drop the subject right now." Good as her word, she sat back and sighed heavily. "Why don't I get my materials together so we can go over the information before we get there?"

"Okay."

"Great." She stood up and leaned down to whisper conspiringly, "This will give me an excuse to get away from Kenny." I laughed and watched her stroll back up the aisle.

The trip to Chicago turned out to be interesting. Snow began falling the moment we arrived; it was early December, so we should have expected the snowfall. We spent the afternoon in meetings, going over the company's software in greater detail than the last time we were there. The company's software had survived the first round of interviews, and now we were taking a much closer look.

The weather began getting treacherous long before we were finished, so we were forced to return to our hotel early. The hotel seemed completely empty when we checked in. Even the lobby and bar were unusually quiet.

We spent the evening laughing and joking with the bartender and waiters. I watched with glee as Sara fended off the advances of two salesman-types that wandered into the bar. She wasn't budging an inch, and I loved watching her quick wit as she jousted with them. It was obvious to me that she found them distasteful, and she played into that, enjoying my amusement.

Eventually we found ourselves at the pool table, playing "men against the gals," as Frank put it. While I loved billiards and wanted nothing more than an opportunity to wipe the smirk off Kenny's face, I hadn't played in years. Sara, on the other hand, had never played. It wasn't very pretty as we went down in defeat game after game.

Somewhere along the line Kenny began to slur his words and tried his best to convince Sara to make a small wager with him. He had propped himself up against the pool table and was rubbing chalk on the end of a pool cue when he finally went too far. "C'mon, Sara. If I win, we go to *my* room. If you win, we go to *your* room!" he bellowed and began to laugh hysterically.

I wanted to choke him. The alcohol wasn't doing me any favors, and I had to work hard to control myself. As I held myself back, I slid a glance at Frank who was shaking his head and frowning.

When I glanced back, Sara took a sip of her drink and approached Kenny slowly. Her smile glittered as she placed a hand on either side of him on the edge of the pool table and leaned into him seductively. He leaned down just a bit so that she could whisper in his ear.

What is she doing? For a brief moment, I thought she had lost all of her senses. Surely she wasn't wasting her time on this egotistical bastard.

The triumphant smile drained from his face as

Sara finished what she had to say and stepped away. "I think I've had enough pool for one night," she said aloud, looking first at Frank and then at me. "Care to join me for a cup of coffee before we turn in?"

I know my smile was wide. "I'd love to," I replied, barely able to contain myself as I watched a sneer curling on Kenny's lip.

"I'm afraid I'll have to pass," Frank chimed. "You two go ahead." He turned to Kenny and reached out for the pool cue. "Time to hit the sack, kid. I think you've had enough."

I watched to make sure they had left the lounge before I joined Sara in one of the booths. Two steaming mugs were on the table between us as I sat down.

I whistled low. "He's such a jerk." I picked up one of the mugs and placed it to my lips.

"He's a dick," she stated flatly.

I choked on my coffee, desperately trying not to spew the beverage all over the table. When I recovered, I looked at her and laughed.

"Excuse me?"

"He's a dick," she repeated, straight-faced. "Did I offend you?"

"Absolutely not." I laughed again. "I'm just not used to hearing women say things like that." *Straight women, that is*.

She wrapped her hands around her mug and stared into it, her bottom lip tugged down at one corner. "Why does he have to act like that?" she asked. "I hate it when shit like that happens. He is so full of himself that he can't believe every woman doesn't want him." She lifted her eyes to mine. "He's the jerk. Then when I set him straight, I get the reputation for being a ball-buster."

"A ball-buster? You?" I was surprised at first, but then I thought about it. I didn't really pay much attention to office gossip, but I began to recall hearing about several guys that Sara had turned down. *A cold bitch.* That was the phrase they'd used.

She was nodding, her eyes a little wider than usual, a little sad.

"Who cares what they think?" I didn't have the slightest idea how to cheer her up. "Fuck Kenny. He was being a jerk. Even Frank thought so."

She tried to laugh and change the subject, but a few moments later she decided to turn in and left rather abruptly. With a heavy sigh, a heavy heart, and a slightly groggy mind, I found myself ambling down the deserted hallway to the elevators. I managed to find my room and was just pulling my sweater off over my head when there was a knock on the door.

I froze instantly, suddenly certain that Kenny was up to no good. I peered through the peephole and looked squarely into Sara's eye.

With a laugh, I swung open the door and stepped right into a snowball that splattered cleanly across my face. I was blustering, speechless as I wiped the snow from my face. A screech of laughter and dashing sneakers were careening down the hall, and I wasted no time in hot pursuit. I chased Sara down one corridor and up the next, both of us slowed by our own giggling. She would have gotten away had the elevators cooperated. But I caught up with her and had her cornered. She slipped to the floor, laughing so hard that tears were streaming down her cheeks.

"Gotcha, gotcha, gotcha!" she giggled. She lifted her arms as if to fend me off. I reached down to grab her. *Grab her? To do what?* I caught myself and pulled back, realizing suddenly that I was about to make a terrible mistake. *Oh great,* I thought, *what am I going to do now that I've caught her? Tackle her? Tickle her? Kiss her?* I sobered instantly and squatted down instead.

"It's okay, you're safe this time," I assured her with a smile as her giggles subsided. "I'll just wait until you aren't expecting anything, and then you'll get your payback."

"That was fun," she smiled, then took a deep breath and exhaled loudly. "I'm pooped."

"Me too." I smiled back as the elevator doors slid open. "You're lucky that elevator is empty. I'd like to see you explain your way out of this one."

She looked down at herself, sprawled on the floor in the hallway of a Marriott hotel. "I guess this isn't very dignified, huh?" She wrinkled her nose and held out a hand. "Help me up."

I stood up and carefully tugged her to her feet. "Don't forget, when you least expect it . . ." I taunted.

"I can hardly wait." She grinned and stepped into the awaiting elevator.

I stood back and watched the doors slide shut. "Wait!" I shouted. The doors magically opened again.

"Yes?" She smiled sweetly.

I stepped closer, nearly leaning into the elevator, and lowered my voice. "Just what did you say to Kenny back there."

She grinned, her tongue doing that tuck and dip thing that I liked so much. "I told him," she drew out the words slowly, "that he could take the pool stick that he was fondling so provocatively and shove it right up his ass."

I threw my head back and laughed loudly.

"And they say I'm a ball-buster," she shrugged sarcastically, her tone incredulous. "Can you imagine?" She let the doors slide shut again as I remembered to call out.

"Good night, Sara!"

" 'Night, Leslie!"

With a satisfied grin, I whistled all the way back to my room.

Chapter 3

The holidays were just around the corner, and I hardly noticed. We were slightly ahead of schedule with the project, and the approaching holidays made everyone a bit more agreeable and inclined to reach a joint decision. We finally made our selection while huddled together on a plane going home to Boston late Friday night, just eight days before Christmas. I spent that weekend with Susan and her lover, Pam. They had waited for me to help pick out the Christmas tree and decorate. While my heart wasn't really in it, I appreciated their efforts. I joined them, going through the motions, trying desperately not to obsess about my future and lack of direction.

On Monday I was back on familiar ground, regrouping with the team to go over the details of the presentation we'd be giving to our CEO and the rest of upper management. In the end, it fell upon me to open the meeting and provide an overview of our investigation and the results we'd be presenting. Along with Frank and Kenny, I then sat back and joined the others as Sara took center stage. Every now and then we were called upon to offer up statistics and figures when needed, but the focus of the presentation was squarely on Sara.

I had watched Sara in this environment on a number of occasions and had no doubts that it was one of her true strengths. But this was the first time that I watched with growing pride and admiration. Perhaps my judgment was becoming clouded, but I don't think so. Sara had an amazing ability to step in front of a group and wrap a special charm around her audience. She was able to take the topic of software, a usually dull subject, and make it seem magical. She knew just how to paint a picture, lead an audience down a path. She knew when to smile, when to interject humor and above all, how to smooth ruffled egos and answer tough questions without appearing overbearing or arrogant.

In the end, I was convinced that it was Sara, and not the software product itself, that was the star of the meeting. It was a complete success, and everyone agreed that we should move forward with the purchase as quickly as possible.

The meeting adjourned, and everyone filed out, thanking us and congratulating us on all of our hard efforts. Sara and I were left alone in a suddenly quiet room. She looked at me, sighed heavily, and jokingly wiped her brow.

"Whew, I'm glad that's over."

"You were incredible," I told her, beaming. I wanted for a brief moment to reach out and hug her. Of course I didn't. "How did you ever learn to talk in front of people like that?"

"I don't know." She shrugged and stepped closer, sitting down in one of the chairs that surrounded the conference table. "But I'm exhausted."

"I can't believe how good you are at speaking like that. You had them all right here." I pointed to the palm of my hand. "I get nervous just thinking about talking in front of a group."

She brushed my compliments aside. "Do you think we sold them?"

"You know you did."

She laughed. "Yeah," she mused, "I guess so." She was thoughtful for a few moments. "It's kind of a letdown, though. After four months of being in high gear, we do this silly little dog and pony show for the big wigs, and then what?"

"Well," I sat down in the chair across from her, "that depends."

She cocked her head to one side, curious.

"Assuming that they actually go through with this acquisition, the next step is selecting a team who will learn everything there is to know about the software and the people who might use it. It will probably mean spending a few weeks in Chicago, training." I stopped and felt my heart swell as a slow grin spread across her face. "Then, of course, that team would have to come back here and work together, installing, testing, training other people. Then there's repackaging, selling, training clients. There's no end, really. Interested?" I asked.

"Of course. This is our baby and I want to be the one who delivers it!" she laughed and then stopped short. "You're still going to be involved, aren't you?"

"Absolutely. I've actually been a little depressed that it might be over," I admitted. "I'm glad you still want to be a part of it. After all," I teased, "playing pool in Chicago just wouldn't be the same without you." We were on cloud nine for the rest of the week.

Against my better judgment, I was quite smitten with Sara. I even let her convince me to attend our annual Christmas party, which always before I avoided at all costs. I arrived at the party alone and was instantly uncomfortable. When I found Sara, she was hanging on the arm of a tall, dark-haired man whom she introduced as James. Warning bells went off in my head as I felt familiar jealousy rising inside of me.

She convinced me to join them at their table. She was going out of her way to be gracious and entertaining while I tried my best to behave and look like I was enjoying myself. I swallowed my pride and danced with James, just to appease Sara and make her happy. I hadn't been on a dance floor with a guy since high school, but I managed to smile and shuffle my feet for a full three minutes, all the while wondering what the hell she saw in this guy.

I made my exit shortly thereafter. My resolve to get out of there didn't waver even when Sara pouted. I was completely ashamed of myself. How could I keep lying like this? In one evening, I had compromised principles that had taken me years to develop. I felt like a teenager. The next few weeks were spent kicking myself, reminding myself of who and what I was, and doing everything possible to quell my growing infatuation with Sara.

By mid-February, contracts were signed, the buyout was completed, and I was on the road again. Sara and I were banished back to Chicago, where a particularly brutal winter was in progress.

I poured myself into work, putting in ridiculous hours, intent only on absorbing everything I possibly could about the software. The training was grueling, leaving little time for anything else. Our off-hours were limited to an hour or two each night. While Sara and I spent most of that time together, it was somehow different from before.

The Christmas party had served as a wake-up call to me. I remembered the pain of coming out to people who couldn't cope with it. I thought of my brother who hadn't spoken to me in nearly seven years. I remembered the friends whom I had trusted and lost. I had been lucky though, compared to so many of my friends. The rest of my family accepted me completely, and I had managed to maintain a few friendships with a couple of straight women who knew I was gay. But I wasn't going to allow myself to suffer another loss. Not now. And I knew somehow that continuing with Sara as I had would only cause pain.

My defenses were up, walls neatly in place. Sara sensed the change, and it saddened me. I could see the question in her eyes and expression. I had silently pushed her away, and she was both hurt and confused.

We were far less playful than before. No midnight dashes down hotel hallways. We laughed and joked, spoke about our work and about politics. We debated. We even argued. But we rarely talked about anything personal. While we did talk a lot about family and what we had been like growing up, I didn't ask her about James or other boyfriends that she mentioned. And whenever she broached a topic remotely uncomfortable for me, I avoided her eyes and her questions. I had, over the years, become remarkably good at answering one question with another. I maneuvered every personal question back to her. If she was catching on, she wasn't letting me know.

The topic of double dating came up exactly twice. The first time, I managed to make some quip and change the subject. The second time, however, I'd had enough and told her so. "I am not even slightly interested in going out with any man, regardless of how well you think I'd like him."

She was stunned by my tone and responded with silence. Then she followed with, "That guy must have really hurt you."

My reply was a groan, and the topic was dropped for the last time.

Throughout those weeks I remained outwardly calm and controlled, while inside of me raged a battle. In the quiet moments before sleep each night, I would lie awake, mulling over the turmoil I was feeling, weighing my options over and over.

It wasn't even a matter of my attraction for Sara. It was much simpler than that. I liked her. I cared about her. And I hated lying to her. I wanted so much to be honest and get that one thing out in the open between us. I wanted her to know that I was a lesbian so that we could move on. But each time my mind was made up, my resolution would crumble.

I didn't want to lose her. Worse, I didn't want to suffer the humiliation and rejection that I felt certain would come. I'm not sure if that certainty was based on a real evaluation of our relationship or on past experience. Either way, I remained frozen, unable to get the words out.

I telephoned Susan nearly every night, exasperating her with my inability to come to terms with my dilemma. It was simple to her.

"Look, just tell her."

"What if she can't handle it?" I'd whine.

"She'll be fine," she assured me yet again. "And besides, if she can't handle it, then her friendship isn't worth the energy that you're pouring into it."

"I know. I just don't want her to hate me."

Susan was patiently impatient. "Leslie, you're a mess."

"I know." I was especially obsessive knowing that after seven weeks, our time alone was nearly over. Pretty soon we would be returning home to Boston once again, and I wanted us to deal with any problems while we were away from the office.

"You've either got to deal with it or let it go."

"I know."

"So what are you going to do?"

"I don't know."

Susan's groan would have amused me under different circumstances. Unable to choose action, I chose not to choose. Instead I played the endless game of weighing the choices over and over in my mind until I was exhausted, and disgusted, with the process.

In the end, Sara forced the issue. On our very last evening in Chicago, we decided to go out to celebrate. We ended up at what had become our favorite Mexican restaurant, and I was trying desperately to appear upbeat. Inside I was depressed and panicking. As much as I kept telling myself to spill my guts, I knew I couldn't do it.

We took our time over dinner, chatting lightly and sipping margaritas. When the waiter cleared away our dinner plates, Sara hesitated only a moment before ordering another round of drinks. "I'm not ready to call it a night," she explained, and I silently agreed. I didn't want the night, or our time alone, to end.

The fresh drinks appeared before us and Sara toyed with a straw, slowly stirring her drink.

"Look, I know there's an imaginary line that I'm not allowed to cross. But I'm going to take a risk and cross it anyway. We're leaving tomorrow, so what can it hurt. Right?"

I took a long and dangerous gulp of my margarita, my thoughts beginning to spiral. She leaned forward over her drink and lowered her voice.

"What happened, Leslie?"

"What do you mean?" I feigned ignorance, but she brushed my feeble attempt aside.

"We hit it off so well last fall. I really thought we were friends. I just don't understand what happened. What changed? Did I say or do something wrong?"

My heart was sinking. Her green eyes were actually bright with tears and bewilderment. Her voice was heavy with sincerity. "No, Sara. You didn't."

"What is it then? I don't get it. I thought we were getting close. Then you clammed up on me. What did I do?"

"You didn't do anything. Really, Sara. It's me." Whether she knew it or not, she'd found my weak spot. I was instantly vulnerable.

"Then tell me what's been up with you. My god, you've been so distant."

"Look." I tried to get the words out, but couldn't. "I can't —" I just shook my head and stared at her, watching the emotions flicker across her face. Sadness, frustration, even a hint of anger.

She sat back, silently watching me, evaluating me. I stared back, helpless, wanting nothing more than to rescue her.

"I've been lying to you." There. I'd spit it out. The first few words. There was no backing out now. Air rushed in my ears as my heart pounded wildly.

She watched me quietly, waiting for me to continue. I needed prompting. She seemed to be searching her memory, but was unable to come up with anything.

"What could you possibly have been lying about?"

Deep breath. Heart pounding. *Say it. Say it. Say it.*

"I'm gay." The two words came out in a whoosh, just barely audible. I cringed and braced for her reaction, reprimanding myself for choosing the word *gay* instead of *lesbian*.

A smile jumped to her lips. A worried one found mine. My relief was fleeting. She laughed loudly and leaned forward. "Excuse me? I thought you said you were gay."

I could feel the blood draining from my face as nervous shivers threatened me.

"I did," I mumbled.

The smile froze on her lips. Her tongue darted out and in. She kept her eyes fixed on mine.

"You're gay?"

I remained focused on her smile, noting how one corner twitched ever so slightly. She was trying desperately to mask her feelings.

"Yes."

The silence that followed was deafening. We sat there for an eternity, simply staring at each other. I was cringing but completely focused on her face and the empty, carefully-fixed smile that remained plastered on her lips. She had been completely unprepared for my confession, caught so off guard that she had no idea how to respond. It was equally apparent to me that she did not like what she had heard but was trying desperately not to show it.

I wished that I could take back my words. I needed to soften the blow. Perhaps humor was best.

"Should I tell you that I'm just kidding?"

Her short laugh was not amused. "Not if it would only be another lie."

Ouch. That was that. I could feel familiar hurt beginning somewhere in my belly. I looked away from her, unable to meet those steely eyes any longer.

She picked up her drink and calmly placed the straw to her lips, sucking long and slowly until the glass was empty. I had never seen a margarita disappear so quickly. She motioned to the waiter and tapped her glass. He complied quickly, taking away the empty glass and replacing it with a fresh one.

I shivered slightly and took a deep breath, letting the cold knot settle in my stomach. This scene was far too familiar to me and, without thinking, my coping mechanisms fell into place.

"So, I guess this explains why you didn't want to double date with me and James," she stated with a raised brow, the smile never leaving her face. I wasn't sure if the joke was sincere or if I detected sarcasm in her tone. It didn't matter. I was now firmly prepared for the worst, and the last thing I would do was let her know that what she thought mattered to me in the least.

"That would be the reason. Yes," I nodded. "I am sorry that I didn't tell you sooner. I wanted to." I shrugged, wanting to explain but not being able to. "It's difficult since we work together."

"And you thought I'd tell everyone."

"Something like that."

She shook her head quietly. It was her turn to put the walls up. I could no longer guess her thoughts.

"I won't do that."

"Thank you." We both sounded so cold, going through the motions. Thankfully, the controlled smile had left her lips. Now her expression was carefully blank.

"I'm glad you finally told me." Her tone was matter-of-fact.

Again I tried humor. "That makes one of us." This time her smile was wry. I thought she might let me off the hook, come to my rescue somehow. But she didn't. We simply sat silently. Out of nowhere, anger engulfed me and I wanted to hurt her the way she was hurting me. I tried to check my anger as I watched her finishing her new drink. She must surely be feeling the effects of the tequila.

"Maybe I should be the one to drive us back to the hotel?"

The eyes that met mine weren't quite focused. "That would probably be a good idea."

I watched her for a moment, giving her another opportunity to say something, but she didn't. "Okay then, let's go." I stood up and dropped a wad of bills on the table before turning away. Sara followed a few seconds later.

Chapter 4

If our friendship had grown a little cold over those last few months, then my confession had plunged it squarely into a deep freeze. The next morning, we checked out of the hotel in awkward silence. The ride to the airport was thankfully short, and I drove again at her request. Her only words were, "I will never drink another margarita as long as I live," before she slipped sunglasses over her eyes and leaned against the back of the seat.

With little time to spare, I dropped her off at the

terminal before returning the rental car and boarding the plane. I was disappointed, though not surprised, that Sara was not in her assigned seat next to mine. I spotted her a few rows back, huddled in the corner and staring out the window. I debated whether to say something and was about to approach her when she caught me staring.

"I think I want a window seat today." Her voice was carefully polite.

"You can take mine. I don't mind the aisle."

She shook her head and motioned me away. "No, no. You go ahead. I'm probably just going to sleep anyway."

I stood staring down at her, bursting inside, wanting to scream and shake her and make her understand. I wanted to tell her that I hadn't changed, that I was still the same person that I was six months ago. But I couldn't. I just stared down at her, willing her to reach out. But she turned away, obviously uncomfortable, and stared out the window. My knees grew weak and my eyes clouded over as I stumbled back to my seat.

Over the following weeks Sara's rejection was complete. The blank smile and polite voice became the standard with which she addressed me. We avoided each other whenever possible, our interaction limited to meetings when a group of others were around us. Our gazes never met, and she made it perfectly clear that she no longer wanted a personal relationship with me of any kind.

Those first few days I spent in something like a stunned stupor. I knew the shock had worn off when I spent a solid week kicking myself before anger took over. I allowed it to settle inside me, cynicism replacing my bruised ego. *Another lesson*, I told myself. The same old lesson, learned all over again.

My eventual change in attitude began to show in the way that I responded to her coldness. I couldn't help the occasional sarcasm that slipped into my voice, and I stopped caring whether or not my mocking responses were noticed. She was the one who had cast the die, and she would have to deal with the consequences.

The next phase in our project also helped to put distance and perspective between us. My duties now shifted to the technical side completely as I worked with Frank and Kenny to bring the software to Boston and install it on our computers there. We then began the tedious process of making changes to the system, coding and testing, making improvements wherever we thought they were needed.

Sara, on the other hand, was charged with the unenviable task of finding a business partner for our company. The idea was to find a highly visible company willing to cut a deal with us. We would completely overhaul their existing computer system and replace it with our own at no expense to them; in exchange, we would use their name as a reference and in our advertising strategies. It was a relatively common practice in our business.

Sara practically jumped at the opportunity to get back on the road again. As a result, she was out of the office three or four days a week, wooing potential customers.

Near the end of May I was able to get away for a vacation on the Cape. I tagged along with Susan and Pam to Provincetown and spent the next ten days lying on the beach under a blistering sun, floating in the cold Atlantic salt water, and picking my way over pebbled beaches.

In those two short weeks, Sara managed to close a deal with the Austin Group, a prestigious retail chain based in Atlanta, Georgia. When I returned from vacation, we met with two men who represented their company. The first, an older gentleman named John Austin, had started the company some forty years ago. His one-room store had grown into a chain of furniture stores all across the southeast.

The other gentleman could not have been much older than myself. Billy Austin was John's grandson, and it was obvious that he would one day inherit his grandfather's business. It was equally obvious that Billy Austin was gay, particularly when he appeared more than casually interested when I mentioned where I had vacationed. We hit it off instantly.

The next several months were filled with anxiety as we worked long distance to hammer out a proposal and a contract. During that time I was in constant contact with Billy, who turned out to be incredibly talented and outrageously funny. We developed an easy, teasing friendship.

By August, tension had grown between our two groups, to the extent that no one really believed that a deal would be made. So when Billy called for his daily chat just two weeks before Labor Day, I reached for the phone with reluctance.

"Hey, gal," his throaty drawl called out before the receiver was pressed to my ear.

"Surprise, surprise," I laughed. "Hey Billy. Got any real news for me today?"

"It's done."

There was silence as he waited for my reaction.

"No. Are you kidding?" After weeks of stagnation, I couldn't believe it.

"No kidding. I just faxed you a signed contract."

I chuckled, enjoying the moment. "I can't believe it."

"Believe it," he implored. "When can you be here?"

"Whoa, Billy. We haven't even picked the team yet."

"That's easy. We know who we want. You and Sara. Period."

Although somewhere in the back of my mind I had known I might have to spend some time in Atlanta, the thought of traveling again left me exhausted.

"Gee, Billy," I hedged. "I'm really not sure. I'll have to work on it here and get back to you."

"Ah c'mon, Leslie." His voice dipped lower as he teased me. "You'll love it down here. I promise I'll show you a heck of a good time."

"Yeah, I'll bet you will." While we hadn't actually come out to each other, I was certain that he knew I was a lesbian.

"Seriously, Leslie. I want this to go as smoothly as possible, and I am confident that you're the best person for the job."

I chewed on my bottom lip for a moment. "And Sara?"

"Well, Sara managed to charm an awful lot of people while she was here. She would certainly help smooth the transition."

I thought about what he was saying, knowing it

made sense. But I dreaded the thought of working that closely with Sara again. I didn't think I could stand her coldness day in and day out.

"I'll talk to her, Billy. We'll work something out."

"Okay. Call me tomorrow and let me know when you'll be here." He laughed, full of himself, and hung up the phone.

Well, well. I certainly am in a pickle now. I placed the phone back in its cradle and gazed out the window, wondering just what to do next. I knew that I had to formulate a plan before my boss got too involved. He would bend over backward to make Billy happy, and I wanted to avoid an embarrassing scene with Sara.

I decided that the best thing to do was swallow my pride and confront her with Billy's idea. Together, maybe we could come up with a plan of action.

With much trepidation I found myself outside the door of her office. I took a deep breath and peered in to find her, thankfully, alone. She was sitting at her desk, dark head bent over several charts and graphs that were spread out before her. A pair of glasses were propped on the end of her nose, and an errant lock of hair fell low on her forehead.

I watched her for a moment, slightly wistful. I missed her. The old her. But I was thankful that I had been able to put it behind me. Before my nerves got the better of me, I tapped lightly on the open door.

Startled, she glanced up, whipping the glasses from her nose and dropping them on the desk.

"Sorry to bother you."

"It's okay." She recovered quickly from her start

and fixed a smile on her face. I was sincerely beginning to hate those perfectly even white teeth. "What can I do for you?"

I wasn't sure how to start, so I decided to forget the preliminaries and dive right in. "We might have a problem, and I thought it best that you and I should try to come up with a solution before someone else does." She didn't offer me a chair, but I sat down anyway. "The good news is that Billy called and the contracts have been signed. So congratulations," I added awkwardly.

Her eyes sparkled as a slow grin spread across her face. She really was quite beautiful. "We did it." I sat quietly and let her soak up the news. After a moment she continued. "I'm glad. So what's the bad news?"

Here I stammered a bit as I explained. "Billy was specific about whom he wants in Atlanta for the installation. He was quite adamant, actually."

"He wants you and me to do it," she said quickly.

"How did you know?" So this wasn't a surprise after all.

She shrugged. "He's made it clear to me practically since the day he met you."

"You talk to him a lot?"

Again she shrugged. "Quite a bit," she admitted, settling back in her chair and entwining the fingers of both hands together. "I don't know why it should surprise you so much that he wants you and me to do it." She allowed herself a moment of arrogance. "After all, you can't blame him for wanting the best."

I watched her cautiously, not trusting her.

"So what are we going to do about it?" I asked carefully.

"What do *you* want to do about it?" she shot back. "Actually, I'll admit that I always thought we made a pretty good team," she added evenly. Now she really had me at a disadvantage. Was she being serious? I couldn't read her, so I decided to ignore her last comment.

"I'd like the opportunity to see this thing through. But not if it's going to be uncomfortable. It's not worth it. We would have to work together day in and day out." I paused briefly. "And it wouldn't look good if we can't manage to get along. In public, at least." I threw in the last part as a dig.

She cocked her head to one side. "So we'd be forced to behave ourselves. Is that what you're saying?" I knew she was taunting me, but I wouldn't give in.

"Something like that."

She sat back quietly for a moment, watching me evenly. Appraising me. I returned her gaze without blinking.

"Sounds like a challenge."

"No, Sara. No challenge," I sighed, suddenly tired. "I'm just tired of conflict."

She nodded. "Okay. Billy wants the best, and we'll give it to him. And I'll try very hard to behave myself."

"That's it?" The resolution had been too easy.

"As far as I'm concerned it is. We both want to be a part of this project, right? What else can we do?"

Uncertain, I stood and walked to the door. "So

41

that's it?" I asked again. "I can tell Billy and Dennis that we'll do it?"

She laughed, not answering my question directly. "On the road again . . ." she began to sing, her voice low and twangy.

I held up my hands. "Okay, okay. I'll put everything together and get back to you."

She nodded, still singing. I made my exit and sauntered down the hall, replaying the conversation in my mind while trying to figure out what had just transpired. A truce of sorts, I decided. But I wasn't trusting her for a minute.

Chapter 5

We arrived in Atlanta on the Tuesday after Labor Day, our uneasy truce having managed to stick throughout our preparations for the trip. So far, Sara and I were able to work together in a strictly professional manner, each of us carefully masking any of the personal feelings she might be having.

Sara had told me that I would love the accommodations in Atlanta, but I wasn't prepared for the plush beauty of our hotel. The Austin Group was located in Buckhead, a suburb of Atlanta, and the Ritz-Carlton was within easy walking distance of their offices. The company kept several rooms there for visiting clients, and Billy had insisted we use them while we were in town.

It was a gorgeous hotel. Our rooms were near the top floor, on the east corner, overlooking the pool area. I laughed silently to myself when I discovered that a connecting door joined my room to Sara's. Susan would definitely get a kick out of that, I decided, thinking that under different circumstances, its existence would have been quite amusing.

The first two weeks were filled with meetings as we met with various individuals to develop a strategy for converting the systems. As if the days weren't long enough, the members of the Austin Group were intent on filling our social calendar as well. A different cocktail party was planned on our behalf nearly every evening, and our attendance was more than encouraged, it was expected. It didn't take long before the nightly parties created far more stress for me than did the long days of work.

While Sara was in her element, smiling and gracious with each introduction, I struggled with the endless greetings, chatter, and questions. With each new introduction came the obligatory welcome and the inquiry about our personal lives. I hated those questions and, worse, I hated the way everyone pointed out single males for us to meet.

To Sara's credit, she came to my rescue whenever possible. She created a line about me being married to my work that she used on anyone who got too nosy. I never thanked her for it, although perhaps I should have. She probably could have derived some sadistic pleasure from watching me squirm under everyone's scrutiny.

44

At the first cocktail party, Billy had swaggered up to me and placed an arm around my shoulders, hugging me to his side. "I'd be willing to bet that you hate the questions about being single as much as I do," he whispered next to my ear.

I looked up into his huge blue eyes and wrinkled my nose. "And you would definitely win that bet," I laughed.

After that, he rarely left my side. He sympathized with my predicament and laughed. "Honey, they gave up asking me when I was going to get married a long time ago." He confided in me that almost everyone knew he was gay. "They like to pretend they don't know," he shrugged.

After nearly three weeks, on a Thursday night, even Billy had begun to lose his good humor. We were seated in the lounge area of the hotel, just the three of us, watching from a distance as a number of coworkers laughed and joked among themselves.

"Well, the good news is that you gals have met just about everybody in the entire corporate office," Billy drawled as he swirled the ice cubes in his drink with one finger.

"That's good news?" I asked.

"It means they're running out of excuses to have another one of these wingdings. With any luck, this will be the last one." He paused for a moment, looking tired. "Are you two heading back to Boston this weekend?"

Sara nodded. "Tomorrow night around six." So far, Sara had made it back each weekend.

"What about you, Leslie?"

"Hopefully. We'll see how it goes tomorrow." Unfortunately, I had only been back once. It had been a brief visit to pick up more clothes.

Sara clucked her tongue and turned to Billy. "What are we going to do with her, Billy? She's all work and no play."

"Yep," he played along. "I hear she's married to her work."

Sara cackled. "Who did you hear that from?"

"Besides yourself? Nearly everyone."

"Gee," I tossed in. "I'm certainly glad that word is getting around."

We grew quiet until Sara snapped her fingers and leaned forward, a mischievous gleam in her eye.

"That's it!" She looked from one of us to the other. "All work and no play!" Billy and I just looked at each other.

"Billy, take us away from here. Surely you know someplace that we can go for fun." She tapped his knee lightly with her fingertips.

A naughty grin slid across his face. "Honey, I sure do. Let's do it."

"It's ten o'clock," I pointed out. The last thing I wanted was to get in a car and go out to some bar. At least here I was only moments away from my bed.

"Don't be a poop," Sara admonished me and quickly downed her glass of wine.

"But won't everyone miss us?" I knew I was whining.

We all glanced around, noting that the lounge was definitely thinning. I barely recognized most of the faces.

"No one that counts," Billy muttered, lifting his tall frame from his chair. He winked and smiled warmly at Sara before extending his hand out for mine. "Come on, darlin', Sara wants to go out and play."

I muttered under my breath as I gave him my hand.

Within moments of parking the car, I realized that Billy had brought us to a gay bar. I looked around and noticed same-sex couples moving through the parking lot toward what appeared to be the back door of a club. I held my breath and waited for Sara's reaction, but she didn't seem to notice. Or rather, she noticed but chose not to mention it. She seemed oblivious, joking and laughing on Billy's arm as they walked a few steps ahead of me.

Once inside, it would have been impossible for Sara not to know where we were. The first room held a quiet, room-length bar with stools. A number of drag queens huddled at one end of the bar, their voices loud over the sound of music that pulsated from another room.

Billy led us through that room to another, and then another, waving and greeting women and men alike as he went.

"Popular guy," Sara noted, lifting her brows. I nodded, barely able to hear her as we got closer to what I assumed would be a dance floor. Finally, we stepped through a doorway and found ourselves in a dimly lit room, littered with tables and chairs that

47

surrounded a dance floor. Four drag queens were out there now, lip-synching to an old Diana Ross and the Supremes hit.

I couldn't help but smile. It had been far too long since I had been in a place that equaled this one. The dance floor was three steps down from the table area. Above me, I could see a balcony of sorts where other people sat at more tables, looking down over the drag show.

Billy settled us at a table off to one side, slightly away from the direction of the deafening speakers.

"Like it?" Billy called, wiggling his eyebrows for my benefit.

I had a wide grin on my face as I nodded. "I sure do."

Sara replied as well, but I couldn't hear what she was saying. He asked each of us what we'd like to drink and turned to the waiter who had materialized at his side. Billy obviously knew him too.

I tried not to look at Sara as I sat nervously, wondering how she was reacting.

"Uh, I assume those are men out there." She leaned close to my ear so that I could hear her.

I followed the direction of her eyes and watched as the song ended and another began, the queens not missing a beat.

I looked at Sara and nodded.

She went back to watching them, completely absorbed. "They're good," she called, just loud enough for me to hear. Her eyes drifted from the dance floor to all the people who swarmed around us. I looked around, trying to see everyone through her eyes.

Surely she saw the gay couples together, laughing and flirting. And kissing. She seemed to be handling it okay, so I decided to relax and enjoy myself.

Drinks arrived and the drag show ended. I noted that Sara's applause was as enthusiastic as my own. The speakers thumped as country music blared and couples moved out to the dance floor.

Soon a number of Billy's friends began dropping by the table. He introduced us to every one, and Sara became animated and chatted with them as I took the opportunity to scan the crowd.

We had been there for some time when my eyes fell on a small, dark woman squatting on the steps directly across from us. She was laughing and calling out to a couple who were two-stepping.

People danced in and out of my line of vision, and each time they did, I strained to find her. For a full song I watched her blissfully, until the song ended and couples began shuffling between us. I was searching frantically for her when my eyes finally focused on her again. Relief gave way to panic as I realized that she was staring right back at me, her eyes unwavering as she smiled. I checked myself, uncertain. *Get a grip, Les. She's probably staring at Sara.*

My stomach fluttered as I watched her smile.

"Leslie. Yoo-hoo, Leslie?" My eyes snapped around to Billy, who was trying to introduce me to yet another of his friends. We shook hands, and then I tried not to appear too obvious as I swung my head around to find the dark woman again.

My eyes flew to the steps, to the dance floor, to

the tables across the way. Too late. I had lost her. *Damn.* My eyes began to wander, darting from one table to the next as I tried to find her.

"Leslie. Leslie!" I felt Billy tugging at my sleeve, trying to get my attention.

Where is she? I abandoned my search momentarily and turned to Billy.

My eyes grew wide as I saw her, leaning over just enough so that her face was inches from Billy's.

Billy's eyebrows were dancing as he introduced us. "Leslie, Sara, this is Michelle." He drew her name out slowly.

"Hi," she smiled, her teeth white against her dark complexion. She acknowledged Sara with a nod, then extended a hand to me. "You're Leslie?" Her eyes moved back to Sara, "and Sara." We both nodded, although I could only see Sara from the corner of my eye.

"Nice to meet you," I murmured as I shook her extended hand.

"You aren't from around here," she stated, holding on to my hand a bit too long before releasing it. I looked away, then quickly met her dark eyes again.

"They're from up north, honey," Billy interjected. "Boston. They're going to be in town for a few months doing some consulting with my company." He leaned closer to her, pretending to whisper. "You'd better work fast, honey. They won't be here for long." Again the eyebrows were dancing, this time at Michelle. Her laugh was throaty as she grimaced at him.

"You'll have to excuse my friend's rude behavior.

50

Billy has a one-track mind." She leaned down to whisper in my ear conspiringly. "Don't worry. We're not all like him down here."

I laughed, flushing as I felt her breath on my neck, causing goose bumps to threaten. As she tilted her head away from mine, the lights caught her hair. All I could see was black, black crisp hair. Black, black eyes laughing into mine. For a moment, I forgot that Sara was even in the building.

"Join us," Billy insisted, borrowing a chair from the next table and planting it firmly between him and me. Michelle hesitated only a moment before sliding in to the chair.

I was suddenly claustrophobic as I found myself stuck between the two women, unable to leave the table without getting by one of them. I was very aware of each one and I wasn't sure which one made me more nervous.

Michelle was hot, no doubt about it. I found myself staring blatantly at her profile while she chatted with Billy. Her hair was indeed as black as I had thought, almost shiny. It was thick and short, with stylish soft waves. Her voice was rather deep, and when she smiled, a small pucker appeared on her left cheek, too high to be considered a dimple. I guessed her to be a few years younger than myself.

"You're not blinking." Sara's voice floated quietly into my left ear. I jumped and turned to meet assessing green eyes. One eyebrow was raised. I couldn't quite read her expression. Questioning? Mocking? I could feel the heat rising in my face. "Or breathing, either." Her tone now definitely mocking. "Breathe, Les, before you pass out." She picked up my wine glass and placed it in my hand. "Have a drink." I took a big sip as she leaned a little closer, making sure she was out of earshot to the others.

"Well, well, well," she tsked. "Tell me, is she your type?"

"Only in my dreams," I muttered under my breath. I wasn't sure if Sara heard me or not. I took another drink and nearly choked when Sara elbowed me. Smiling sweetly, she inclined her head toward Michelle when I slid her an annoyed look. I turned to see that Michelle had shifted, her attention directed toward the two of us.

"How could you tell that we weren't from around here?" Sara leaned forward on the table, her upper body leaning across me so that Michelle could hear her better.

"No accent," Michelle replied, then changed her voice to mimic a southern twang. "Most folks from down here in 'lanta have an a-ac-cent."

"What about you? You don't have an accent either."

"I'm from Phoenix originally. I came to school here and haven't found a good reason to leave."

The two of them bandied chatter and laughter for some time. I began to phase out, barely listening as I watched. Back and forth, from one to the other. I was aware of each's perfume, her laughter, her eyes. I nursed my drink carefully, thankful that I had a few moments to gather my wits. It was then that I literally choked when I heard Michelle's question.

"You two are not a couple?"

I coughed hard and shook my head, my eyes darting wildly to Sara, who was taking the question quite calmly.

"No, we're not. We're friends." She patted me on the back and looked at me quizzically. "Are you okay?"

"Just fine," I replied, putting on the best nonchalant face I could muster.

"Did you leave anyone special behind when you came down here?"

Sara harrumphed and shook her head. I simply said no.

"Good," was her reply. I looked at her quietly to be certain. Yes, she had definitely directed the comment toward me. A number of Billy's friends chose that moment to swoop over to the table, becoming loud and distracting us from our conversation.

The music changed from country to a popular dance tune, and everyone left tables behind for the dance floor. Michelle leaned closer, her eyes burrowing into mine.

"Thank goodness! I hate country music," she smiled. When I agreed with her, she reached for my hand. "Dance with me."

A slow panic began to rise in me. Dance? I hesitated as I replied, "Uh, I don't know. I don't think I've drunk enough to make a fool out of myself." I tried to joke, knowing it was lame.

She smiled anyway, then snapped her fingers as if she just had a brilliant idea. "Don't go away. Good thing this is a long song." She jumped from her seat and threaded her way to the bar.

"Where'd she go?" Sara interrupted her other conversation to ask.

"To get a drink."

"Is she coming back?"

"I don't know." I looked up and watched Michelle turn away from the bar, a glass of wine in her hand. She raised the glass and grinned when she saw me watching her. "I think so."

"My, my. You sure work fast," Sara teased just as Michelle placed the drink in my outstretched hand.

Michelle stood beside the table, looking down at me. "Okay, drink up. I did my part." I sighed and took a long sip. "C'mon, the song's nearly over." She glanced at Sara momentarily. "You don't mind, do you, Sara?"

"Not at all," she replied in her polite business voice. *Of course she wouldn't mind. Why would she mind?* I glanced at her briefly and shrugged before following Michelle out to the dance floor.

I was terribly self-conscious. I took a few moments to acclimate myself by moving side to side very simply as I observed the woman before me. I was surprised to note that she was shorter than I am by several inches. She was solid, but petite. Before long I couldn't help myself, so I had to ask.

"Why ask me to dance instead of Sara?"

She cocked her head to one side. "Two reasons. One, I don't mess with straight women."

I was incredulous. "How did you know she's straight?"

She shrugged. "Sixth sense. You can't tell me that you don't have it too?"

"You're right. I usually do." We moved around the floor a little before I laughed and drew closer to her. "I thought maybe you came over so you could meet her."

"Then why would I be dancing with you?"

I shrugged. "Too shy to talk to her?"

"I don't think so!" She shook her head and laughed at me. "I assure you that if I want to talk to a woman, I don't usually dance with someone else just to get up the nerve."

I gave her an appraising look. "No, I don't suppose you do," I laughed. "What was the second reason?" I asked.

She replied but I couldn't hear her. "Excuse me?" I motioned that I couldn't hear her. Michelle reached out both hands and grabbed mine, tugging me closer as she called, "Because I think you're very attractive."

Flustered, I looked away and happened to catch Sara's observing eye. I didn't look back at the table again.

We danced. Uncertain at first, trying to find the rhythm. I fell into a side-to-side shuffle. Feeling stiff and awkward, I focused on Michelle's body. The song was a light, flirty tune, and her movements matched it. She was playful and teasing, having fun, and a wonderful dancer. Watching her was at once inspiring and seductive. I grinned happily and was rewarded by her unabashed smile and a particularly delightful move. Magically, everyone else in the room receded.

For a brief moment, I stopped moving and stepped back, hands on hips. She laughed as I scrutinized her moves. I continued to watch her, feeling the music, and stepped in closer. The real dancing began. I followed her moves, delighting in my ability to keep up. It was so incredibly exhilarating. I giggled as she raised her eyebrows and widened her grin. "You can dance!" she called, surprised. I wasn't offended.

We didn't miss a beat as the song changed,

slipping into yet another wildly popular song with a heavy beat. The song expressed seduction, passion, and just a hint of raunchiness. Our movements reflected the change.

Michelle spun away now, appraising me. She grinned, tucking her bottom lip between her teeth as she stepped forward and into my rhythm. She was in front of me, then behind, all the while her body hovered against mine. She teased, she taunted. Her movements matched, then countered my own. We continued to play the game. Smiling. Laughing. Nearly wrapping around each other, in and out, but never quite touching. Our bodies reacted and followed, smoothly, subtly, blatantly, heatedly.

The song faded out without the usual mix of a new one. The emcee sashayed out to announce that another drag show was about to get underway. Michelle booed loudly before turning and bowing neatly before me. "I could have danced with you all night," she called before giving me a quick thank-you hug.

"That was fun. I never get to dance like that any more. Thank you." I was completely sincere, wishing that the music had continued longer. On impulse, and completely uncharacteristic of me, I dropped a quick kiss on her cheek. I was exhausted, but happy.

"Will you come back then? Another night?" The crowd was thinning, making room for the show to begin.

"Of course. I'd love to."

Billy hooted from the table. He was whistling as we got closer, pointing at the two of us, hooting and throwing catcalls. Then he and Michelle began teasing each other as my face grew redder and reality set in.

I didn't dare meet Sara's eyes as I slid into the chair beside her. *What must she be thinking?*

"Well, you certainly didn't dance like that at the Christmas party last year." Sara's voice had that mocking lilt.

I groaned inwardly and met her eyes, fully expecting to suffer the brunt of more teasing. She was smiling at me over the rim of a wine glass, one eyebrow raised.

"I haven't danced like that in years." I felt defensive, exposed, and terribly uncomfortable.

"Then you should do it more often."

Was that a compliment?

She shook her head slowly and tsked with her tongue. "I had no idea." she mused.

What did that mean? I felt a warm hand on my elbow and turned to find Michelle's dark eyes inches from mine. "It's getting awfully late. I have to work tomorrow, so I have to leave now."

"Hmm." I glanced at my watch. Nearly one o'clock. "Yeah, we should probably be leaving too." Her hand was resting on my forearm now.

"Will you tell me where you're staying? We have a date, right?" She smiled hopefully.

"Of course. The Ritz in Buckhead."

"Ooh, very nice," she purred playfully. "No room number?"

I laughed a bit uneasily. "I don't like to give out my room number . . ." *As if I so often had occasion to do so.*

"I understand. I'll call then, okay?"

"Great. Thanks again for the dance and the drink."

"Entirely my pleasure." She squeezed my hand

and gave me a final smile before saying goodbye to Sara and Billy and threading her way toward the front door, waving to many as she went.

The drive back to Buckhead was a relatively quiet one, with Billy monopolizing most of the conversation. I tried not to squirm too much as I fended off his comments and questions about Michelle. Sara remained strangely quiet.

Sara was also noticeably absent the next day. I put my ear to the adjoining door, hoping that the silence on the other side didn't mean anything. But she never appeared after breakfast. It wasn't until after noon that Billy ran into me and mentioned that she had taken a morning flight back to Boston for the weekend. I don't think he noticed my anxiety or confusion.

God. Last night must have really put her off. *You really blew it this time, Les,* I chided myself. *Blew what? It's not as if there was something to blow.*

"I did hear from Michelle today, though," Billy told me. "She wanted to call your hotel but didn't know your last name. I hope it's okay that I gave it to her."

"Of course." My thoughts turned to Michelle, and I decided that if a message was waiting when I got back to my room, I wouldn't bother returning to Boston that weekend.

Chapter 6

I wasn't disappointed. Michelle had left a message just after three o'clock, and I wasted no time returning the call. We agreed that she would pick me up for dinner at seven-thirty, and I found myself humming once the phone was firmly in its cradle.

With two hours to kill, I paced nervously, wondering what I would do as I waited. I decided to call Susan. Although she was initially disappointed that I wouldn't be coming home, she was excited when I told her about Michelle.

"You dog," she teased.

"She's hot, Susan."

"My type?"

"Your type. My type." We continued to banter for a while and, before finally hanging up the phone, I assured her that I would tell her all the details.

I waited until precisely seven-thirty before leaving my room and heading for the elevators. Michelle was lounging in a chair to one side of the lobby, smiling slowly as she watched me approach. I took a deep breath, wondering how she managed to look even better than I'd remembered. She was dressed simply in black pants and a short-sleeve white cotton blouse. Her thick short hair looked unruly, as though she had just run her fingers through it. A thin gold chain winked at me from her throat.

"Hi." She smiled as she unwound her small body and stood.

"Hi." I swallowed hard, hoping she wouldn't notice my nervousness.

She led me outside and into the evening breeze, making polite conversation as we walked. We ended up at a small Italian restaurant in downtown Atlanta, where the aroma of herbs and garlic was nearly as intoxicating as the bottle of red wine that we shared.

I needn't have been so nervous. Michelle was charming and entertaining, and she went out of her way to put me at ease. She spent the first hour telling me amusing stories about her first few years in college at Georgia State. I realized, as I listened, that there was a time in my life when I would have considered her too outgoing, too gregarious for my own tastes. But now, I found her incredibly appealing.

"What have you been doing since then?" I asked her. "College, I mean."

She wrinkled her nose, her cheek dimpling. "I haven't decided yet what I want to do. I have a degree in physical education." She grinned and lowered her voice. "No dyke gym-coach jokes, okay?"

I laughed.

"I thought about teaching for a while, but I'm uncomfortable with the thought of going back into the closet. Know what I mean?"

"I sure do."

"I'm enjoying myself and biding my time while I can afford to do it. But I'll have to decide sooner or later." She took a sip of wine and continued. "Right now I'm doing part time work to get by. I tend bar at the club where we met the other night, and I also give golf lessons at a local country club."

"Golf lessons?" My ears perked up. I loved golf.

"Six days a week." She nodded. "You play?"

"Not well and not often. But I love golf."

"Great. Maybe you'll play with me while you're here?"

"I'd love to." I looked down at the small hands that were wrapped loosely around a wine glass. My eyes traveled up her forearms and rested on the softly outlined muscles. I wondered why I hadn't noticed before.

"Tell me how you met Billy," I asked.

"He used to work out in the gym at my college while I was a TA."

"You've known him for quite some time then."

She shrugged. "Only about a year and a half."

I did some mental calculations and was a little

confused. She was in college a year and a half ago? Suddenly it dawned on me.

I squinted and leaned across the table. "Just how old are you, may I ask?"

She grinned a little sheepishly. "Twenty-three. Next month."

"Ha!" I sputtered. "You're a baby!"

"Oh, come on. Twenty-two isn't that young. How old are you?"

I grimaced and shook my head, envying her all the more. No wonder she seemed so carefree. "I'll be thirty-four before the year's over."

"Ooh, an older woman." She grinned and wiggled her eyebrows.

I was appalled. "I am hardly an older woman."

"And I am hardly a baby."

I sat back for a moment and grinned, completely enamored.

"Touché," I retorted, and was rewarded with her throaty laughter.

We sat talking over coffee far longer than either of us realized. It was just after ten-thirty when she grimaced. "I can't believe it's this late."

"We talked for hours."

She smiled, resting her chin on the knuckles of her left hand. Her dark eyes stared into mine.

"You're easy to talk to."

"You are too." I felt the nervousness from earlier returning.

She sighed heavily, sounding tired. "I hate to say this, but I have a golf lesson at six, and I need to get some sleep."

"We should go then."

She nodded and paid the bill before escorting me to the door.

We were relatively quiet on the short drive back to Buckhead. When we arrived at my hotel, she stopped the car at the end of the circular driveway and cut the engine, turning to me as she shut off the headlights.

My stomach began to flutter. *Uh-oh.*

Without meeting my eyes, she reached over and picked up my left hand and held it in hers. She traced my palm for a few moments before lifting her eyes to mine. I noticed how much darker they looked from just minutes ago.

"I don't want to say good night."

Uh-oh. Stay calm. "I had a nice time. Thank you."

She looked at me quietly, then wrinkled her nose.

"I don't suppose you want to invite me up?" she asked hopefully, almost shyly.

"You have a golf lesson at six," I reminded her, surprised at the calm in my voice.

She looked a bit disappointed, but recovered quickly. "Hey, we could play golf tomorrow afternoon. Maybe go dancing tomorrow night? What do you say?"

"Yes." I didn't even have to think about it.

She seemed relieved. "Good. How's two o'clock? I have to work until noon."

"Perfect."

"Good." Awkwardly, she hesitated before leaning over and pressing her lips against my cheek. Then she leaned back just enough so that she could look up at me through her lashes. I watched as she closed her eyes and leaned forward, pressing her lips to mine. It was a slow, soft kiss, tasting of garlic and wine.

Reluctantly, she pulled away, her eyelids heavy.

"I'll see you tomorrow." Again she sighed.

"Okay." I let myself out of the car, shut the door firmly behind me, and leaned down to look through the open window. "Thanks again. Good night."

"Good night," she smiled as the engine turned over, and she slid the car into gear, waving briefly before heading out into traffic.

Michelle was right on time again the next day, this time looking adorable in her golfing duds. It took us just over a half-hour to get to the country club, where she outfitted me with clubs and shoes.

"How long do you think you'll be working down here?" she asked.

"Initially I thought about three months. Now I think it will be more like four altogether."

We laced our shoes and journeyed out to the first tee. She offered to get us a cart, but I said I'd rather walk. I enjoy the sound of golf cleats on pavement, and I grinned at the sound as we crunched across a little bridge that ran from the clubhouse to the course itself. It was after three o'clock, and the course was relatively empty.

I was shy at first, knowing that I hadn't held a club in over a year. Michelle was patient, though, encouraging me and giving me pointers throughout the day. She had a beautiful stroke, and I respected her talent immediately.

"Wow. How did you ever learn to hit the ball like that?" I asked after a particularly spectacular drive.

She waited until the ball landed on the fairway some two hundred plus yards away before she replied. "When I was a little girl, my dad used to take me to the driving range just about every day." She bagged her wood and heaved the bag over one shoulder as we strolled toward our balls. "He used to say there was nothing sweeter than the thwack of a well-hit ball."

I chuckled. "Are you and your dad close?" We reached my ball, and I held out my bag. "Which club?"

She looked out toward the green and shook her head. "You'll need your three iron." I probably wouldn't get near the green even with a three.

She stood back and waited quietly for me to swing. I was surprised when the ball fell within a couple feet of the target. I turned to Michelle and smiled. "Not exactly a thwack," I said. "But not exactly a kerplunk either."

She laughed and we began walking forward again.

"So, are you close to your dad?" I asked, continuing our conversation.

She let a few moments pass before replying. "Not anymore." Her voice was flat. "He's a politician. Local stuff. City councilman, that sort of thing," she explained. "He wasn't too wild about his daughter being a dyke. He sent me down here to school, and I haven't been back since. We have an understanding. He sends me a big fat check every month, and I don't go home." She shrugged. "I figure I won't see my folks again until after he retires."

My heart sank a little. "I'm sorry," I told her.

"Don't be," she said as she steadied an iron beside her ball as it lay in the rough. The ball popped into the air and ran onto the green, stopping just two inches shy of the hole. She grimaced as she looked at me. "Close," she sighed, then stepped over and tapped the ball into the hole.

I watched her as she retrieved her ball, and she stopped when she caught me watching. She straightened up and looked at me steadily. "It really doesn't bother me much anymore. Besides, if it wasn't for him, I wouldn't get to do this every day." Her arms swept out as she indicated the golf course around her.

I let the subject drop as I focused on my next shot. The ball skidded and bounced, running far beyond and to the right of its intended destination. It was hopeless. Two putts later, I finally put the ball where it belonged.

After eighteen holes of golf, I was discouraged by my score. It was nearly twice what Michelle had shot.

"Perhaps you should consider professional lessons." She grinned broadly as I unlaced my shoes in the empty clubhouse.

I laughed. "Perhaps I should."

"I make house calls," she teased, her voice barely above a whisper.

I stopped what I was doing and looked at her, caught off guard by her sudden flirtation. My mouth hung slightly open as I eyed her. She grinned again, and bent over to cover my mouth with hers in a brief, thorough kiss. I looked around quickly to make sure no one had heard the loud smack, which brought another chuckle to her lips. "Don't worry. Everybody here knows about me."

I went back to changing my shoes, thinking hard about her comment. In my best southern drawl, I asked her, "You bring a whole lotta gals here, do ya ma'am?"

"Why, never a one before you, I swear." She batted her eyelashes in southern belle imitation.

I eyed her speculatively, and my voice returned to normal. "Yeah, I'll bet."

After a brief dinner at a local deli, we drove back across town to the gay club. I tried to convince Michelle that I should go back to my hotel to change, but she insisted that I not bother. "Besides, if we go back to your room, then it's likely that I won't want to leave," she told me sweetly before reaching over and slipping her hand into mine. I continued to be surprised by her innuendos, even as they became more frequent.

It was early when we arrived, only nine o'clock. The place was quiet. No music was playing, so all I could hear were conversations, laughter, and clinking glasses.

We settled on a table beside the unlit dance floor, and I soon found out that everyone, it seemed, was a friend of Michelle's. She was even more popular than Billy had been the other night, and I found myself surrounded by both men and women. Michelle introduced me to each and every one as the jokes and laughter and alcohol flowed.

Over the next two hours, the place began to fill up, becoming even more crowded than it had been that previous Thursday night. At precisely eleven o'clock, the dance floor was lit, the speakers thumped into life, and the drag queens began their show. I enjoyed myself immensely. By midnight, the show was over and the dancing began. Michelle and I danced nonstop for a solid hour before falling back into our seats, tired and sweaty.

Michelle ordered another round of drinks for our table, and I finished mine easily. "I'm exhausted," I called above the music.

She placed her hand on my thigh and leaned her head close to mine so that she could hear me.

"Me too." She smiled and sipped her drink, leaving her hand on my thigh.

"Do you work here a lot?"

She shook her head. "Usually three or four nights a week. I have to work tomorrow night."

Another glass of wine was placed in front of me, courtesy of one of her friends. I took a sip, feeling reckless and knowing that I'd already had enough to drink. I turned to Michelle and told her as much.

"Is that good or bad?" she asked coyly.

"Bad, I think. I'm not very good at drinking."

"Is that because you get sick or because you lose control?"

I was astonished by her straightforwardness, and I laughed. "What do you think?"

She tipped her head to one side and smiled at me. Her eyes looked so dark again. My eyes dropped to her mouth, and I watched her sip her drink slowly while she assessed me. She licked her lips quickly, and I decided that I wanted that mouth. It had been too long.

She leaned in closer until her face was inches away, her eyes looking directly into mine. "I think," she began, "that it's because you're afraid that you'll lose control. And you don't trust yourself when that happens."

I stared into her eyes, mesmerized. I could feel the effect of the alcohol washing over me. She was right, of course, but I didn't answer her. I couldn't answer her. I was completely focused on her eyes, her mouth, her eyes again. Her mouth.

"Do you ever lose control, Leslie?" I could barely hear her voice, but I knew exactly what she had asked. My eyes flew to hers, searching. I knew she was sucking me in, teasing me. But I didn't care.

Before I realized what I was doing, my hand was at the nape of her neck, pulling her closer until my mouth covered hers. No softness this time as our mouths opened, our tongues meeting hungrily. My fingers slipped and twisted into the thickness of her hair as I urged her closer, closer.

Our kiss broke as quickly as it had started, and we stared at each other before she smiled sardonically. "I guess you do," was all she said.

Back to my senses, I blushed and looked quickly around, knowing that at least a dozen of her friends had seen the kiss.

We left soon after that, and I stumbled out to the parking lot, feeling tipsy, knowing I would reprimand myself in the morning. She had her arm around me as we made our way, and I leaned into her just a bit. We reached her VW, and she carefully swung me around to face her, grabbing both my hands and placing them on her hips. She held me, gently pushing me back until I was leaning against the car door.

My mind swam as she began to kiss me, the full length of her body pressing into mine, straining to get closer. Our mouths were open, sucking, searching until I could focus on nothing else. Then her hand was on my breast, teasing through my shirt. My entire body was suddenly alive as electrical currents coursed over me, through me. *Oh god!* My knees grew weak, but she caught me, held me up with one arm, slipping a leg between mine, creating more pressure.

My breathing was heavy as she continued to tease me. Her mouth was on my neck now. Biting, nibbling. Causing tingles to slide up and down my spine. *Oh my, my, my!*

"Michelle?"

A familiar male voice fell on my ears, causing me to stiffen instinctively. I ducked down a little so that Michelle was standing in front of me, one arm still around me as she turned toward the voice.

"I thought that was you." I knew the voice. It was Billy. "Gee, I'm sorry, doll. I didn't realize . . ."

"Your timing is awful," Michelle told him, her voice husky.

I peeked over Michelle's shoulder and cringed a little when I saw his bearded jaw drop.

"Leslie?"

"Hi, Billy." I waved sheepishly.

"Oops, sorry." He raised both hands apologetically. "Didn't mean to interrupt." He stepped backwards. "Just pretend I wasn't here." He smiled, embarrassed, and turned away.

We watched him walk away before Michelle turned back to me.

"We should probably go now," I said, and she nodded in agreement.

"I'm really sorry about Billy," she told me when we were back at the hotel, parked at the end of the horseshoe driveway.

"It wasn't your fault. Don't worry about it." My head was clear now, the mood of the moment definitely gone. I knew that she was disappointed, but I couldn't help it. She didn't ask to come inside. Instead she told me that she wished she could see me tomorrow, but she had to work. "What about Monday?"

I shook my head regretfully. "Work night. I don't know how late I'll be."

"Friday?"

"If I don't go home for the weekend," I laughed. "You certainly are persistent."

"Only when it's worth it," she replied.

I kissed her softly and thanked her before saying good night.

I spent most of Sunday swimming and lounging by the pool. I stretched out in the hot sun and let my mind wander. Last night had left me with a severe case of sexual frustration. I had almost forgotten what it felt like. But it was there with me all day, that dull ache that just wouldn't go away. I allowed myself the luxury of replaying the events of the last night, relishing the memory of Michelle's mouth and the thrill of her practiced hands.

She certainly knew exactly what she was doing, I chuckled to myself, speculating that Michelle was no stranger to sexual encounters. I imagined she had probably had more than her share of women in her young life. I, on the other hand, had never quite been able to let go and appreciate sex with someone unless I believed that I was in love with her. While part of me was proud of that fact, another side of me occasionally wanted to break out and discover what it would be like to be carefree.

I imagined what it would be like to sleep with Michelle, squirming just a little as I lay on the lounge chair. I rolled over and put my face in my arms.

I had no misconceptions about where this new relationship was going. I knew very well that it wasn't about falling in love and living happily ever after. I was certain that Michelle wasn't looking for that sort of thing. Just as I was equally certain that for me, it was more of a physical attraction than anything else. So far.

It felt good to be wanted. Pure and simple. Particularly by someone as young and attractive as Michelle. The question was, could I get sexually involved with her without getting too emotionally involved? After all, I would be returning to Boston in a couple of months. The last thing I wanted was to be pining away for someone.

The question rattled around in my mind for several minutes until I decided that my heart was probably pretty safe with this one. But I knew there was only one way to find out for sure. I made a silent pledge to let go a little, to enjoy myself, and Michelle, as much as I could.

By four o'clock I'd had enough of the sun and headed back to my room. I started thinking about dinner, then thought perhaps I should spend some time writing letters that evening. I let myself into my room, the fragrance of freshly-cut flowers greeting me as I did. A huge bouquet of roses, carnations, and baby's breath had been placed on the table. I smiled and approached them to lean down and inhale deeply. A small card was tucked into the arrangement, and I pulled it out and opened it up. It was simply signed *Michelle*. My smile grew. It was nice to know that she was thinking about me too.

I decided to call and thank her, hoping that I could catch her before she left for work. I was in luck.

"They're beautiful. Thank you," I said when she answered the phone.

"You're welcome." I could hear the smile in her voice.

"When do you have to go to work?"

"Actually, I'm on my way out now."

"Oh. I'll let you go. I just wanted to thank you."

"Okay," she hesitated. "Listen, if you're not doing anything later, you can always come down to the club. It's usually pretty quiet on Sundays, and you could keep me company."

"I have to work tomorrow," I told her.

"Ah well, can't blame a gal for trying. Can I call you before Friday?"

"Of course."

"Then I will. Talk to you soon."

We said goodbye, and I hung up the phone, feeling a little depressed. *What did you expect? That she'd take the night off?*

I took a shower and ordered room service. While I watched TV and wrote letters, the scent of the flowers occasionally wafted over me. By nine o'clock I'd had enough. I changed quickly and called a cab.

It was nearly ten o'clock when I reached the bar. Someone was shouting "Last call," and I flew from room to room, not knowing where, or if, I'd find her.

I finally spotted her in the main room overlooking the dance floor. I stopped dead in my tracks when I saw her, astonished again by her striking beauty. She was behind the bar, leaning against the counter and idly wiping the inside of a glass with a towel. The cuffs of her long-sleeve white shirt were rolled back to expose her forearms. A black bow tie hugged her neck, matching a short vest of the same color. She was lazily watching two couples on the dance floor moving to a slow love song.

I slipped along the side of the bar until I was beside her. She hadn't noticed me, so I grinned and leaned over the counter as far as I could.

"Do I still have time to order a drink?" I asked.

Startled, she swung around. Her surprised smile was all I needed to see. Any second thoughts I might have had vanished instantly.

"I can't believe it." She reached out to grab my hands in hers. "I'm so glad you came."

"Me too."

She filled a wine glass and slid it across the counter to me. Then she pouted a little as I took a sip. "It's late. The place is nearly empty, so we're closing in ten minutes."

I nodded. "I know."

"Maybe we could go for coffee?" she asked. "I know you have to work tomorrow. I wouldn't keep you out long." Her eyebrows were raised with hope.

My eyes traveled over the dark skin of her face. Her hair was tousled again, and her eyes were bright. Her mouth was . . . calling me.

"Coffee would be nice," I told her.

"Good." She grabbed a towel and brushed it over

the countertop, then ducked beneath the counter to step out and stand beside me.

"You know," she whispered in my ear as her arms slipped around my waist, "I hear the coffee at your hotel is absolutely fabulous."

I laughed softly and lifted my arms until they circled her waist. I buried my face in her hair and inhaled deeply.

"You're absolutely right. It is." I leaned back to see her eyes as they looked into mine. "But actually," I began, swallowing my nervousness, "the coffee that they serve in the dining area isn't nearly so good as the coffee served in the rooms."

Her eyes grew wide with surprise. Her smile couldn't have been any bigger than my own.

"Room service? Hmm. Is the coffee just as good in the morning?"

"Even better," I promised.

"I can't wait." With a grin, she tossed the towel back on the counter, grabbed my hand, and led the way through the crowd and out to the parking lot.

Chapter 7

Michelle was an incredible lover. Ardent and insatiable one minute, laughing and playful the next. We barely slept and I was exhausted before I even got to work the next morning. I hadn't even sat down in my chair before Billy popped his head around the corner and wished me a loud and singsongy good morning.

"Good morning to you," I replied, sheepishly recalling the last time I had seen him.

"I'd be willing to bet that one of us had a very pleasant weekend." He grinned suggestively as he stepped into the office and settled into a chair. My face flushed as I stumbled for a reply. "I really am sorry about the other night," Billy continued. "I hope I didn't spoil anything for the two of you."

I finally found my voice. "We somehow managed to salvage the weekend," I assured him, keeping my voice low but playful.

"Ooh, I'd love to hear all about it. But I'm afraid I've got bad news. The programmers ran into some problems over the weekend. Grandfather got wind of it and is on his way to see you."

"Oh, great." I rolled my eyes. Just what I needed.

"Sorry." He lifted an armful of computer printouts and stacked them neatly on my desk. "Thought you might want to have a look at these before he gets here."

"Thanks." I flipped through them briefly. "From yesterday?" I asked.

"Yep. Once you've had a chance to get a handle on things, give me a call. We can go over everything then."

"Thanks, Billy."

"No problem." He stood up to leave and was almost out of the room before I called out, waving him back in.

"Have you heard from Sara?" I asked.

He shook his head. "Didn't she come back last night?"

Last night? Oh my God! Could Sara have actually been next door last night? And this morning? "I hope not," I muttered aloud.

"Excuse me?"

"Oh," I waved him off. "I don't think so. At least I didn't hear her."

"Are you worried about her or something?"

"Kind of. Yeah." I looked at him hard. "Sara didn't take it well when I came out to her. I'm worried that she might have flipped out when we took her to the bar last Thursday."

"Oh, I don't think you need to worry. She'll be fine." He checked his watch. "She'll probably be here any minute." He hesitated, then headed back to the door. "Gotta go, doll. Good luck with John."

Reluctantly, I watched him go before turning back to the stacks of paper before me. The next hour was spent assuring John Austin that everything was fine. Bumps were expected during a conversion, everything was on schedule, not to worry, and so forth. He wouldn't leave my office until I pointed out that the problem wouldn't get solved if I spent the day talking to him instead of getting to work.

Once he left, I checked my watch. Ten-thirty. Where was Sara? I had a gnawing fear that she had resigned from the project. My anxiety bubbled as I grew more and more certain that she wouldn't return from Boston.

I scooted my chair across the floor and gazed out the window at the parking lot. It was a beautiful day. Gorgeous. A perfect day to play hooky. Michelle's laughter came to mind. So sweet. I had enjoyed her this weekend. Thoroughly. The thought crossed my mind again that Sara might have been in her room last night. I thought hard, trying to remember if I'd heard anything. *Not that you would have noticed.* I rubbed my eyes and blinked, trying to clear the cobwebs. No, the silence from the other side of the adjoining door was deafening over the weekend. I was almost certain that she hadn't been there.

"You sure look awfully tired." Poof. Sara was there beside me, leaning her hands on the windowsill and looking down at me. All smiles. "Rough weekend?" She raised a brow and sat in a facing chair, crossing long legs at the knee and tugging at the hem of the skirt that just barely covered her thighs. There was no mistaking the innuendo in her voice. *Uh-oh. Maybe she had been there after all.* My nervousness quickly changed, replaced with an odd mixture of anger, relief, and frustration. I wasn't in the mood for her repartee. I didn't reply immediately, but held back to check my anger, boldly eyeing her from her legs back up to her face.

"No." I knew my voice had an edge. My eyes bored into hers. "Actually, there was nothing rough about it."

I scored a hit. Her eyes flickered briefly.

"You didn't go home," she stated.

"No." I knew what she was thinking, what she was hinting at. But I wasn't about to let her know. "Why would I want to go home when I can have so much fun here?" I laughed and picked up a computer printout, flipped through it, and tossed it carelessly to the floor.

She actually looked relieved.

"We've got a little disaster this morning, and John Austin just spent the last hour down here quizzing me on deadlines."

"Ouch. No wonder you're a little grouchy this morning."

"Who's grouchy?" I squinted my eyes and growled. "Okay, out you go. That's all the abuse I can take this early on a Monday morning." I stood up and shooed her toward the door. "Why don't you round up Billy and his people and plan on meeting back here at eleven for a briefing, okay?"

"Aye, aye." She saluted me and was nearly out the door before turning back.

"I . . . I'm sorry I took off last week without telling you. I should have let you know that I was leaving."

I nodded and shrugged casually. "It's not like I worried or anything. Or missed you."

"Not even a little?" she teased.

"Well," I conceded, "maybe just a bit."

She seemed satisfied and laughed. "How about dinner tonight? Do you have plans?"

"No plans. Dinner would be nice." She nodded and smiled and started to leave the room. "Oh, Sara," I called her back in.

"Yeah?"

"Did you, uh, just get in? From Boston, I mean."

She nodded. "I came straight from the airport. Why?"

Relief washed over me. "Oh, nothing. I just wondered."

The look on her face said she knew there was more to it than that. "Sure. See you later." She shook her head and stepped from the room.

My heart felt suddenly lighter. Sara certainly had a way of adding a kind of roller-coaster element to my life. But I had to admit I was glad she was back.

The day was a long one. We huddled for hours, tediously going over line after line of code until at last the problem was identified, the resolution agreed upon. It was a weary but satisfied group that left the office just after nine o'clock that evening. I hadn't seen Sara for several hours. She had poked her head into my office just after six o'clock to say she was headed back to the hotel and to wish us luck. As I trudged my way through the hotel lobby to the bank of elevators, I knew the last thing I wanted to do was go out to dinner. A nice warm shower and a soft bed was all I could think of.

As I fumbled to unlock my door, Sara came around the corner at the far end of the hall, dressed casually in T-shirt and shorts, and carrying a bucket of ice under one arm.

"Hey, you survived!" she called, eyes wide as she smiled.

"Barely," I mumbled, trying to manage a smile as she drew closer.

Her brows drew together in a frown as she reached me. "You look exhausted."

"I am," I admitted. "But I think we found all the bugs. We'll know in the morning."

"Good," she nodded. "You haven't eaten, have you?"

"No, but I think I'll have to take a rain check on dinner. I'm pooped."

"But you must be starved. Why don't we just order up? You go change and I'll order room service and join you, okay?"

"Sure." How could I say no?

I let myself into my room, unlocked my side of the adjoining door, and called the front desk for messages. Michelle had called. The home office had called. The home office could wait. I rang Michelle and was disappointed to get her answering machine. I left a brief message, thanking her again for a wonderful weekend. Next, I rummaged around until I found some comfortable sweatpants and T-shirt, then lay on the bed and closed my eyes.

I must have dozed off, because the next thing I knew there was a knock on the door followed by a booming voice calling out, "Room service!" Sara bounded from one of the chairs near the table and intercepted the waiter before I could even sit up. I shook my head to get my bearings, wondering how long she had been sitting there. She ushered the young man in and stood to one side as he laid out two place settings. He fussed around until she signed the check and slipped some singles into his hand.

"I'm sorry. I must have dozed off," I mumbled once we were alone.

"I didn't mind. I'm sorry you're so tired." She waved me over to join her at the table. "I ordered soup and sandwiches. Hope that's okay."

I nodded, still fuzzy, and joined her.

We ate in relative silence. It was quiet, companionable. I realized with a mental shrug that this was perhaps the first time we had been alone that I didn't feel the usual tingling anxiety. Maybe I was getting over her. Or maybe I was just too sleepy and disoriented to care. Or maybe it had something to do with Michelle.

We chatted lightly about the project. I answered her questions and explained some of the problems we'd found. I had just placed the last spoonful of chicken noodle soup into my mouth when she gave a meaningful nod toward the vase of flowers that separated us.

"From Michelle?"

Uh-oh. I sensed Sara's wall slam into place as I blinked, trying to gather my wits. Then I remembered I didn't have to make up a story. She knew I was a lesbian.

"Yeah. Pretty huh?" I managed lamely, attempting nonchalance.

Sara picked up her napkin and pressed it to her lips.

"Look, if it's none of my business, you can just say so."

"No, no." I waved her off. "It's not that. It's just that . . ." Again I struggled to clear my thoughts from the fog. I was so tired. "Look, can I be honest here?"

"Please."

"Okay." I took my time answering, carefully pouring coffee into first my mug then hers. I stirred in some cream, carefully studying the steaming liquid instead of meeting her eyes. "I'm having trouble understanding this change in you. We haven't spent this much time together in, what, six months? An awful lot has happened between you and me and I can't forget all that and spill my guts simply because you've decided you can cope with it now." I took a sip of coffee, more to stop myself from saying something I'd regret than because I was thirsty. I was surprised by the forcefulness of my voice. Surprised that I could say the words. Surprised to find that her rejection still hurt.

"So let's talk about it." Her voice was quiet and calm.

She didn't have to prompt me, the words poured from my lips unchecked. "I spend so much time avoiding questions. For months I tried sidestepping any references you made to my personal life." I paused, wounds opening, and looked at her. "Then when I finally told you the truth, you just shut down. Wham. No more comments. No more questions. Nothing. Barely even a hello." I stood up and took the few steps to the bed and sat down, anxious to put space between us. "I'm a little leery of opening up to you again." I shook my head, not knowing what else to say.

The silence didn't last long.

"Okay, fair enough," she started, taking a deep breath before continuing, a bit unsteadily. "I owe you an explanation and an apology of sorts." Now it was her turn to fidget, stirring her coffee, her eyes only touching mine briefly.

"When you told me that you were a lesbian," she stuttered slightly over the word, uncomfortable with it, "I took it personally." She held up her hand when something like a grunt escaped my lips. "You really knocked me for a loop, and I couldn't handle it. I know now that those feelings weren't quite fair." She struggled to search for words, and I stayed carefully quiet and expectant.

With a deep breath, she continued. "Initially, all I could focus on was that you had been lying to me all along. I couldn't see beyond that or let that go. I was completely shocked those first few days. All I knew was that I had made this really great friend whom I cared an awful lot about, and I felt that I had lost you. I had tried so many ways to get you more involved in my life. Like trying to set up double dates." Her laugh was without humor as she rolled her eyes. "I kept thinking about those stupid dates and the way you kept sidestepping personal questions, and I felt like a fool. You lied and I was so gullible. So humiliated."

"I'm really sorry about that," I told her. "I know it's probably difficult for you to appreciate. All I can tell you is that I struggled constantly with wanting to tell you. But you have to understand that I've lost several friends that I really cared about, and I just didn't want to risk losing you too. I kept thinking that you would be in and out of my life in no time, and that there was no reason to rock the boat."

"I can't imagine what that must feel like. Pretty awful, I guess."

"It is. But it happens so often that I've almost gotten used to it. Just like I've gotten used to the lies." I shrugged. "But eventually I get to a point where the lies are so big that I can't keep up. I know that I have to make a decision. Either I risk it, move on, and the friendship grows or dies, or I continue to lie, keep the walls up, and the friendship withers and dies anyway, because it has to be superficial in order to sustain those lies."

We were quiet for several moments, sipping our coffee.

"I must have disappointed you then, when I behaved the way I did."

I smiled ironically, trying hard not to let old feelings rise up inside me. "Disappointed? No. Actually, I was crushed."

She winced at my honesty. "I'm sorry. I was cruel. I knew I was being a jerk, and I couldn't stop myself." She shook her head. Again we were quiet. I watched as she bent her head, looking at but not seeing her clasped hands. Quietly, she went on.

"My best friend in high school turned out to be gay." I tried not to show my surprise. "The circumstances when she told me were quite different from what happened with you. But for a while after you told me, I couldn't help wondering why two women that I enjoyed so much both turned out to be gay!" She laughed, or tried to.

She looked so lost, and I was torn between wanting to comfort her and wanting to know more about the circumstances between her and her best friend.

"Anyway," she sighed, "I think I'm past most of that now. I've really missed you. I enjoyed being with you so much before. I miss that. I want us to be friends, and I know that means knowing and accepting who you are. I apologize. I hope it's not too late."

A part of me was nearly elated. Had this woman once hurt me? Had I really spent months agonizing over her? If I could learn to trust her, forgiveness would be the easy part. "Of course it's not too late." My smile was tentative. This wouldn't be easy for me, and I knew it.

"Good," she laughed earnestly, taking a final gulp of coffee. "So tell me, do you like Michelle, or what?"

I wrinkled my nose. "Yes. I like her." My voice sounded less than enthusiastic, even to my own ears.

Sara groaned and threw her napkin at me. I snagged it in midair and tossed it back.

"Seriously. I like her. Other than that, I'm not quite sure how I feel about her." I tried to describe my feelings. "She's sweet, fun. A great dancer. Persistent. Very nice."

"Very nice," Sara mimicked me.

"Lame, huh?"

" 'Fraid so." She cocked her head to one side. "Are you going to see her again?"

"Yes."

She laughed. "Like pulling teeth," she lamented.

"I'm sorry, I'm not good at this."

"So I shouldn't take it personally?"

"No." I was thoughtful. "I'm like this with almost everyone. Trust takes a while."

"Guess I'll just have to work on earning it, then. When are you going to see her again?"

"Friday."

Her eyes glittered as she smiled. "Okay. Tell. I'm dying to know. Did you spend the weekend with her?"

Heat flushed my cheeks. I was not going to talk about this with Sara. "Most of it."

"Argh! You are infuriating!" She paced the floor in front of the bed. "You are good at not answering questions."

I shrugged. "Years of practice." In a sense, I was amused and frustrated all at once. I wasn't trying to be a smart-ass. "I'm sorry," I fumbled. "Give me time to get used to this honesty thing, okay?"

I could tell she was still frustrated, but she was willing to relent. "Okay. No more questions tonight. But sooner or later, I hope you'll trust me enough to tell me about it."

"You got it. Now I'm going to kick you out so I can get some sleep. You're making me think too hard."

"Okay, okay. I can take a hint." She threw up

her hands and sauntered over to the door. Before she was all the way through, she leaned back to peek around the corner at me.

"Thanks for joining me for dinner. I know you really just wanted to sleep."

"My pleasure."

"How about breakfast?"

"Your place or mine?" The words were out before I could stop myself. The heat rose in my cheeks. If she noticed, she pretended not to. She clucked her tongue, playing coy. "Surprise me," she replied, and was gone.

"Surprise her," I muttered to myself with a groan after she'd left. I padded over to pick up the dinner tray and carry it out to the hallway. I locked the door quietly, smiling and shaking my head all the way before turning out the light and crawling into bed. For the next few minutes I lay in the dark, replaying the conversation we'd just had.

I tried not to dwell too much on the past. I didn't want to analyze and pick apart the rationale that she had offered. If I was to take her at her word, then she had been hurting too. And it felt good to have at least talked about it. Perhaps it was even good that so much time had passed since it had happened. Time had given me perspective and a chance to put my infatuation where it belonged.

I didn't know if I could trust her yet. But I wanted to. As a cautious optimism settled over me, I snuggled down into the blankets and gave in to my exhaustion.

Chapter 8

Susan, my confidant, was not nearly so forgiving.
"Be careful, Leslie. I don't trust her."

It was the following Thursday night, and she had
called just as I was returning from the office. I
barely had a chance to slip into my sweatpants and
sweatshirt when the phone rang. She wanted to know
all about my weekend with Michelle. I had been
squirming a bit over her questions, so I changed the
subject by telling her about my conversation with
Sara.

"I'm not sure I trust her that much either. But I want to."

"Just be careful. Don't let her hurt you again."

For some reason, I felt the need to come to Sara's defense. "She's not going to hurt me. Really. She's like her old self."

"Do you still have the hots for her?"

My blood began a slow boil. "I do not have the hots for her," I insisted.

"Uh-huh. And you never did."

"If I did, it doesn't matter. I don't anymore." I wanted to drop the subject fast. "How's Pam?"

"She's fine. Don't change the subject."

"Susan," I sighed heavily. "Please. It's okay." I heard a light tapping on the door between my room and Sara's, so I dropped my voice. "She's knocking on my door now, so I have to go."

"Ooh, the adjoining door?"

"Yes, the adjoining door." I was exasperated but didn't really mind her taunting. "I'm letting her in now." I held the receiver to my shoulder with my chin and edged my way over to the door. Sara was on the other side, dressed in a huge oversize sweatshirt and black thigh-hugging spandex pants. She held up a white bag from our favorite Chinese restaurant for my inspection. It smelled delicious. I motioned for her to come on in and held up one finger to indicate that I'd be just a minute.

"I hate to cut this so short," I was saying to Susan.

"Wait! What about Michelle?"

"I'll tell you all about it later." I watched Sara as she pulled little white cartons from the bag and arranged them carefully on the table.

"Promise?" Susan was asking.

"Promise. I'll try to call later tonight, okay?"

She seemed satisfied.

"Okay. Hey Leslie?"

"Yeah?" I adored this woman, even if she was so aggravating.

"I'll bet I was right all along," she said quietly.

"Right about what?" Now what was she talking about?

"About Sara. She probably wants you."

I laughed nervously, hoping that Sara didn't notice. "Very funny. I owe you."

"Bye, Les."

"Bye." I hung up the phone and took the few steps over to join Sara at the table. "Mmm, smells good."

"I hope I wasn't intruding," she said as she handed me a pair of chopsticks.

Why was I feeling so paranoid? "No, not at all. It was my friend Susan from Boston. I'll call her later. Did you get fried wontons?"

"Of course." She tapped one of the cartons, and I quickly reached for it, opening it up and pulling out a wonton.

It amazed me how Sara and I had slipped back into our easy friendship. Subtle changes had taken place since our conversation the other night. This was the fourth night in a row that we were sharing dinner. She had even joined me for breakfast again that morning after admitting that she hated going downstairs and eating all alone. "The men are all on the make even at that hour," she'd told me.

We were once again open and easygoing with each other. Not unlike before. Yet there were differences.

Intangible differences. It seemed to me that Sara had made a decision to invest an enormous amount of energy into getting me to open up and trust her. She was patient and tolerant in her coaxing, seeming to study my responses, digesting them and filing them away.

There was also the gay thing that seemed to hover between us, and I was very aware of this new facet of our relationship. It always seemed to be there, showing up in small nuances. It was almost as though she was watching me differently, watching me to see if she could somehow identify what made me different. She hadn't yet started asking questions about it, but I fully expected them to come.

Once we finished eating, we assumed what had become our favorite after-dinner positions. I hopped onto the bed and settled near the pillows, pulling my legs up and tucking them under to sit cross-legged. Sara stayed in the armchair beside the table, turning it just enough so that she was facing me.

"How did you know you were gay?" she asked out of nowhere, startling me. Then she laughed nervously, her face contrite. "I'm sorry. That came out wrong. I've wanted to ask but wasn't sure how."

"It's okay," I assured her. It took me a moment or two to gather my composure and my thoughts. Part of me wanted to avoid the question and the topic entirely. But I knew I couldn't. I knew I had to open the door a little wider.

"I'm not sure, exactly." Her eyes grew cloudy, and I realized she thought I was trying to wiggle out of the question. "I'm not being evasive," I laughed. "It's just that it didn't happen overnight or anything.

Believe it or not, when I was a teenager I was really boy crazy. Completely over the top."

"Really?" Her eyes grew wide. "You know, the more I get to know you, the more I can't even imagine you with a guy."

"Oh, it happened all right," I assured her as I took another sip of wine. "The biggest difference in my involvement with girls and boys was that the guys were a social thing. And a physical thing too. I was always a very curious little girl." I wiggled my eyebrows as I placed a pillow against the headboard and leaned back.

"But girls were different." I let my mind drift back in time and recall memories that I hadn't thought about in a long time. "I was always more emotionally attached to girls. My best friends were always too important to me. And they broke my heart the way no boyfriend ever did."

"How so?"

"Because they didn't feel the same way I did. For example, when my best friend in high school decided to go out with a boy one night instead of with me to the movies like we'd planned, I was completely crushed." I shook my head as I remembered.

Sara nodded, accepting my explanation. "When did you know?" She moved her chair around and propped her legs on the end of the bed.

"I dated guys all through high school. Then I went to college and fell head over heels for my roommate." I laughed with irony, smiling as I reminisced. "I didn't realize what was happening. I simply developed the same attachment for her that I had with my best friends before."

93

"Wait a minute." She held up a hand. "What do you mean you didn't know what was happening?"

"It's tough to explain. I didn't put a label on my feelings for her. All I knew was that I loved being with her. That we had fun. We did things for each other. You know, silly little mushy things. But it took a long time to realize I had a huge crush on her." I took another sip of wine and emptied the glass. I didn't bother objecting when Sara offered to fill it again. I waited for her to settle back into her chair before I continued.

"She was —"

"She?"

"Julie."

"Julie," she nodded. "Go ahead."

"Julie was like no one I had ever met before. She was from the West Coast, and she wasn't afraid to say or do anything. Now *she* was guy crazy."

"Did you sleep with her?"

"You're spoiling the story."

"Oops, sorry." She clucked her tongue. "Go ahead."

"So with Julie, anything went. She was the most sexual person I had ever known. She loved sex and loved talking about it. She was the first woman I had ever met who actually admitted to masturbating." I laughed hard, remembering the way I had tried so hard to be nonchalant when Julie was ranting and raving about the wonders of self-pleasure. "Julie loved to tell me about her sexual fantasies, and one of them was about being with a woman."

"She told you that?" Disbelief covered her features.

I nodded deliberately. "Oh, yeah. Nothing fazed

her. She had always wondered what it was like to do different things sexually, and being with a woman was one of them."

"She told you that?" Sara's jaw dropped slightly.

"Yes. She told me that, along with a lot of other fantasies. Now keep in mind that I was pretty shy back then and relatively naive."

Sara harrumphed at my words.

"Well," I reconsidered. "Not *that* naive," I admitted. "But I was shy. I spent months trying not to let her know how shocking I thought she was. I wouldn't react, you know?"

"You mean you kept your cards close to your chest?"

"Exactly."

"You do that now."

"See? I told you not to take it personally."

She smirked, and when I didn't pick up the story again right away, she prompted me. "Well?"

"So anyway," I continued. "We were roommates all of freshman year. By Christmas time I was completely infatuated with her. The more she talked about that curiosity of hers, the more I started thinking about it. The more I thought about it, the more I knew that I wanted it. Then one night late in February, we were lying around and she brought it up again. But this time she asked whether I had ever thought about it, and she asked if I was curious too."

The humor had left Sara's face. She was listening intently, completely focused.

"My heart was in my throat. I panicked like crazy because the last thing I wanted was for her to know that I was in love with her. So, as casually as I could, I made some offhand comment about not having thought about it much but that I might be remotely curious." I was becoming animated as I settled into the story.

Sara did laugh now. "This is so *you*."

I wrinkled my brow. Maybe she knew me better than I'd thought.

"I don't remember exactly how it started, but she began suggesting that since we were both curious, we should try it out with each other. Experiment a little."

"I can't believe this. She manipulated you."

"Believe me, I wanted to me manipulated."

"So then . . ." Sara waved me on.

"Then nothing. For two solid months after that, she tortured me daily. And I mean *daily*. We would talk about it, get to the point where I thought it was about to happen, then she would start a philosophical dialogue about the pros and cons. She would come up with reasons why we shouldn't do it. One day she was afraid that it would jeopardize our friendship. The next day she would change her mind and play with me and flirt outrageously. Then she would shut down again." I closed my eyes for a moment and exhaled loudly. "It was awful. I was up then down, up then down. And all the while, I wanted her so bad it hurt. But I wouldn't tell her."

"Why not?"

"Because I was too afraid that if I brought feelings into it, she would be completely turned off and back away. I wasn't about to give her one more reason not to do it." I was frowning as I remembered those tortured feelings.

"So that's it? The whole story?"

"No. Right before summer vacation, she made it

absolutely clear that she had made up her mind. There was no way, no how, she was ever going to sleep with me. She went home to L.A., and I went back to Detroit. I spent the entire summer completely, utterly miserable. I pined away for three solid months. But the good part was that I started connecting everything in my past and how I had felt about my best friends. I figured it all out. I couldn't actually say the words, but inside I knew what was going on with me."

"What did you do about it?"

"Nothing at first. It didn't occur to me that I could meet other women like me. I wasn't focused on the fact that I was a lesbian so much as that I was in love with Julie. She was the only one I wanted. So I waited and waited until we were together again that fall."

"Were you roommates again?"

I nodded. "It was awkward at first. She acted like we had never even talked about it. She went out with one guy after another, and I just kept to myself. I was pretty miserable by then."

"I'll bet." Sara had finished her wine and set the glass down on the table behind her. "Did it ever come up again?"

"Oh, yeah. Eventually we started getting close again. And just when I was getting my hopes up again, she dropped a bombshell."

"What?"

I looked at Sara squarely, the pain of the past nearly choking me. "She told me that she had slept with an old girlfriend of hers over the summer."

"No!" Sara looked stricken. "How could she do that to you?"

"My thoughts exactly. She said that she had still been curious, but that she was able to sleep with the other woman because she didn't mean as much to her as I did. Go figure."

"Oh, Leslie, that's awful."

"It was. I don't know how I got through classes, but I did. And somehow later that year, we finally did sleep together."

"How did it happen?"

"I don't know," I shrugged. "I was giving her a back rub or something, and she started kissing me." I stopped for a moment, rather pensive. "But you know, it wasn't really the same by then. It was a letdown. My feelings were tarnished."

"So wait a minute. What happened after you slept together?"

"The next day I got up and went to class. I was on top of the world. I even stopped on my way home to buy her a rose."

"Nice touch."

"She didn't show up after class like usual. So I waited and waited until finally she came in around midnight. She was evasive. So I gave her the rose." My chuckle was harsh. "She thanked me, then told me that it had been a mistake. She liked men, and it would never happen again. Period. And it never did." I drained what was left in my glass. "And that, my dear, is the end of the story. My one and only experience with breaking rule number one."

"Rule number one?"

"Rule number one," I quoted, "Never, ever get involved with a straight woman." I looked at her furrowed brow and then realized what I had just said. "Sorry. Nothing personal. It's an old lesbian credo."

She chewed on that mentally, then thought to ask, "Did you ever get to tell her how you felt?"

"No. So much happened after that. I still talk to her now and then, but I don't think she ever really knew. Or wanted to know." I stopped and then added as an afterthought, "She's married now."

She stared at me for a few moments, her expression serious. "I'm sorry, Leslie. You must have been devastated."

I admitted that I probably was. "But that was a long time ago." I held out my wrists to show her, trying to lighten the conversation. "See? No scars."

"Not that I can see, anyway."

"Ooh," I groaned, feeling my walls beginning to rise. "You're analyzing me again. I've gotten over most of that old stuff. I'm sure you've got some real horror stories yourself."

"A few, maybe." She smiled at me now, the first time in quite a while. "You're trying to turn the tables on me again, and I'm not falling for it." She yawned and stood up to stretch. "Hey, you've got a date tomorrow night."

"That's right, I do." I smiled back. "Now who's trying to turn the tables?"

"I was just getting used to having dinner together every night." She cocked her head to one side and pouted. "What am I going to do without you?"

My heart skipped a beat. "I'm sure that you'll manage."

She wandered across the room a couple of times, not meeting my gaze. Finally, she reached for the door to her room. "I think, Leslie Howard, that in the future you should try to schedule your dates so that they are a little more convenient for me."

A guffaw escaped my lips. The nerve of that woman! "You're absolutely right, Sara," I mocked, playing her game. "I have my priorities confused."

"I'm glad we got that settled," she teased, grinning. "How about breakfast?" She inclined her head toward her room. "My place. Just for a change of scenery."

"Sure." I laughed, then wished her a good night.

Chapter 9

We ducked out of work a little early Friday
afternoon to go shopping. Sara needed to pick up a
gift for her sister's birthday that weekend, so I
decided to join her, hoping that I might be able to
find a new outfit to wear that night with Michelle. I
didn't tell her why I wanted the new clothes, but it
didn't take her long to figure it out. Soon she was
on a mission, trying to find me just the right
ensemble.

"What kind of look are you going for?" she asked
as we entered her favorite clothing store.

"Something that doesn't make me look fat."

She groaned and rolled her eyes. "No, silly. What kind of look do you want. Fun? Seductive?" She was grinning as she held up a thin, low-cut frilly blouse that wouldn't have covered either one of my breasts.

"Very funny."

She cackled at my response, quite tickled with herself, and put the blouse back on the rack.

"I just want some new pants and a shirt," I told her.

"Do you think you could narrow that down for me just a bit?"

I was beginning to wish that I hadn't decided to tag along with her.

"Okay. Nice pants. Casual, not too dressy. And a long-sleeve shirt, I think. Nothing funky or anything. Simple. Something soft."

"Soft?" she drew the word out suggestively. I rolled my eyes and watched as her fingers brushed across one shirt after another.

"Feel this." She was holding out the sleeve of a bright red shirt. Humoring her, I reached out and slipped my fingers over the fabric.

"Ooh, soft. Very nice."

"Ramie," she told me, and lifted it off the rack.

"I'm not wild about the color, though."

"Me either." She shook her head and put it back, her eyes already scanning the store. With the look of a hunter going in for the kill, she zeroed in on her prey.

"This is it!" Beaming, she pulled down a cobalt-blue version of the red shirt she'd just shown me and held it out for my inspection.

"Much better."

She turned it around and held it to my chest. "Hold it up so I can see."

Embarrassed, I did as she asked, trying not to shrink under her scrutiny. Her eyes traveled up and down, from my face back to the shirt.

"Perfect," she announced, a satisfied grin on her face. "This color is really good on you. It brings out the color of your eyes."

"My eyes?"

"Yeah. They're blue." She tugged the shirt from my grasp and leaned closer until barely six inches separated us. Her eyelids dropped, and she smiled lazily at my discomfort. "I suppose you thought I never noticed." If I didn't know better, I would have thought she was flirting with me.

"Would you like me to tell you some other things I've noticed about you?" Her eyes never left mine as a slow, seductive smile crept to her lips. Her green eyes were bright as she tipped her head to one side, daring me to call her bluff. At least I thought that's what she was doing.

"You're playing with me." The words spilled unchecked, sounding as incredulous as I felt. I could feel the color rise in my cheeks.

"Playing with you?" The grin widened. Sara was feigning ignorance.

"Toying," I offered, relieved.

Her voice dropped even lower. "I wouldn't have the slightest idea how to toy with a lesbian." Her face remained teasing, coaxing.

I watched her for a moment, studying those huge eyes and beautiful white teeth.

"Somehow, Sara," I told her, in a voice that I hoped equaled her tone. "I'm sure you'd do just fine." The words sounded like a challenge, even to my own ears.

Our eyes locked. We were so close I could hear her breathing, smell her light perfume. For the first time ever, I noticed the ring of gold flecks that circled the green of her eyes, the splatter of light freckles across the bridge of her nose. Those full lips, slightly parted, looked so soft, so wet. *If I lean over just a bit . . .*

But her smile faltered and she drew back a little, her face closing. The air seemed heavy, oppressive. The moment was gone. Silence stretched. Uncomfortable silence. I grasped for a way out, to save face.

"I'll take it." I reached out and grabbed the shirt from her hands. "Come on. I still have to find some pants, and you have a plane to catch." I turned and headed for a display near the front of the store, feeling her right behind me as I went.

I settled on a pair of brushed cotton khaki pants and bought both items without trying them on. Sara reacted by telling me that I wasn't being a very sensible shopper, and admonished me nonstop as we made our way across the parking lot and back to the hotel. When we reached our rooms, she insisted that I try on the outfit for her inspection.

"Open your side. I'm coming over," she told me. It had gotten to the point over the last week that the doors connecting our rooms were always open. I flipped the latch on my side and heaved my shopping bag onto the bed. I did a quick check to see if the message light was flashing on the phone, but it wasn't lit. My alarm clock flashed six-fifteen. Michelle would be there at seven.

I could hear Sara behind me, and I flopped down on the bed and turned to face her. "I almost forgot," she was saying, "I need to run downstairs and get some wrapping paper. Want to tag along?"

"No. I've got to hurry and get ready to go. What time's your flight?"

Her eyes flew open briefly. "I almost forgot. Seven forty-five. I'll run down and be right back." I nodded and she disappeared behind the door. A moment later I heard the sound of the hallway door opening and closing.

Once alone, I pulled my new clothes from the shopping bag and laid them on the bed, inspecting them for wrinkles. To my relief, there were no telltale signs that either had just been purchased. There wasn't time for a shower, though, so I stripped off the skirt and blouse I was wearing and slipped into the new khakis.

My thoughts shifted to Michelle and the evening ahead as I scurried about, running a brush through my hair and frowning at the results. It never behaved when I wanted it to. I spent far too much time deciding which pair of shoes to wear, finally settling on a pair of loafers. I was pulling them on when there was a knock on the door.

My head snapped back, and I looked at the clock. Too early for Michelle. Maybe Sara had forgotten her key. *Great.* The blue shirt was still lying on the bed, and the only thing covering me was a bra.

"Just a second," I called, grabbing up the shirt

and fumbling to undo all the buttons as I moved to the door. I pushed my arms through the sleeves and gathered the front together in one hand. Without bothering with the buttons, I reached out with the other hand and pulled the door open.

"Hello there." I must have looked stunned, because Michelle was laughing at my expression.

"You're early," I said flatly, stepping back to let her in.

She closed the door behind her, her eyes never leaving mine. I'd forgotten how dark they were. She looked gorgeous in a light gray blouse tucked into black-and-white checkered trousers. Just seeing her made my hormones race.

"I'd say I'm just in time." Her eyes leered playfully as she reached for me, sliding both hands under my shirt and letting them sneak around my waist to rest at the small of my back. I released the front of my shirt and let it fall open as I lifted my arms and wrapped them around her neck.

"I missed you." I barely had time to whisper before she was kissing me soundly.

"Mmm. It's been a long week," she mumbled against my mouth as she gently guided me backward until the edge of the bed was behind my knees. She eased me down carefully, her lips never leaving mine.

Then she was on top of me, and I knew nothing except the taste of her mouth, the tingle of her fingers as they brushed the shirt farther back from my shoulders. Her lips were on my neck, nibbling and biting, while her hands seemed to be everywhere at once, instantly teasing, arousing. The ache between my legs was immediate, insistent, demanding attention. I tugged at her shirt, needing to feel the softness of her skin. Again her mouth was on mine, falling open as I pulled her down. Tighter. Closer. I took her tongue between my lips, slowly sucking, wanting that fullness in my mouth. Then her hand was at my waist, tugging at the zipper of the khakis without success. I smiled and broke the kiss to reach down and help. I froze.

Sara's face loomed above Michelle's shoulder. She was leaning against the edge of the door that joined our rooms, staring and looking utterly stunned. The moment seemed to last forever. Sara looked wretched, I was unable to move, and Michelle continued to kiss my neck, oblivious. Finally, Sara took a deep breath and shook herself.

"I'm sorry. I —" she stopped in midsentence and fled the room.

Michelle lifted her head, a question on her face. "Sara?"

I nodded. "Shit," I muttered. "I forgot the door was open."

Michelle sat up and I followed, standing to button my shirt. "I've got to catch her before she leaves, okay? I'll only be a minute."

Sara was stuffing clothes into an overnight bag when I caught up to her. She knew I was standing there, barely a foot away, but she wouldn't look at me.

"Sara," I began.

"I'm running late. I really have to get going." Without looking up, she closed the bag and zipped it up.

"Sara, don't," I pleaded. My stomach hurt. My head hurt. Why did she make me hurt so much?

She turned away from me, flinging the bag over her shoulder. Now anger was beginning to mix with remorse. I chased her. "Dammit, Sara. Stop." Completely out of character, I grabbed her by the arm and spun her around.

She looked wounded.

"I'm sorry. I didn't mean to stare." Now she was pleading. Backing away.

"It's okay. Stop it, all right?" I realized I still held her arm and let go.

"I'm embarrassed right now, and I have to catch my plane . . ." She looked so lost.

"I know, I know. Please, don't leave angry with me again, okay?"

"Angry?" She guffawed. "I'm not angry with you, Leslie. Don't think that. Okay?"

The knot in my stomach began to ebb. "Okay."

"I have to go. I'll probably be back Sunday." She began backing away again, and this time I let her go.

"Okay. See ya." I scrambled, not wanting her to go.

She opened the door and paused to look at me. "Apologize to Michelle for me, okay?"

I nodded.

"I guess the outfit was a hit." She smirked lamely, and I tried to laugh as the door closed behind her.

* * * * *

"Is she okay?" Michelle was lounging on the bed when I returned.

"I think so." I sat beside her, and she reached for my hand. "I can't believe it. I looked up and she was standing there. Staring at us. I don't think I've ever seen her so edgy."

"Have you two known each other very long? Are you very good friends?"

I didn't answer right away. How well did I know Sara? Not as well as I liked to think, I decided. We spent so much time talking about me anymore that I hadn't even thought to ask about her. *Some friend.*

"We're friends, yes." I searched for the right words. "But it feels fragile somehow. Like I'm afraid it will break." I shook my head. "We started traveling together on this project about a year ago, and we really hit it off. Then last spring I came out to her, and she didn't handle it well. It's only been the last couple of weeks that we've started to get close again."

"So seeing us lying on the bed together was probably kind of a shock." She tugged on my hand. "Don't worry. She'll get over it." She placed a small hand behind my neck and squeezed lightly. "Do you suppose she likes you? I mean, *likes* you."

My laugh was nervous as I recalled our conversation at the mall earlier that day. "No. Definitely not. She's straight."

"Maybe she's curious?"

For the first time, I allowed myself to think about the possibility. She had been asking a lot of questions lately. "I'm not sure." I was staring into space, and Michelle reached up to tip my face back to hers.

"What about you?" she asked quietly. "How do you feel about her?"

I was reticent to respond. First, I wasn't sure of the answer. And second, it felt awkward to talk to Michelle about my feelings for Sara. She seemed to recognize my hesitancy and smiled.

"Don't worry. I'm not going to fly into a jealous tirade because you care about another woman." She held both of my hands now, her eyes focused on mine. "I think you know where I'm coming from. Don't you?"

I fully appreciated and welcomed her honesty. "You mean you're not going to ask me to marry you?" I pouted playfully. Her laugh was throaty, causing me to like her all the more.

"You said it yourself," she shrugged, still smiling. "I'm still a baby. Too young to settle down."

I pretended to be crushed but kept my tone light. "I'll just have to enjoy you while I can, then." I brushed her lips with mine and sat back, smiling.

She searched my face, a bit uncertain. "You're okay with this? You're not looking for something more serious?"

I chuckled. "Not right now, Michelle. Don't worry. But I have to tell you that this is new for me. I'm not usually like this." I dropped my voice down low, sneaked my fingers into the thickness of her hair and kissed her hard. "I like it."

She pulled me close, crushing me in a long, hot kiss. I was melting.

"We have dinner reservations at seven-thirty," she mumbled, her eyes staring into mine while our lips never parted.

"I'm not hungry," I told her, my entire body screaming for attention.

"I am," she growled. She leaned over and pushed me back none too gently into the soft mattress.

Chapter 10

When Michelle suggested that we spend the weekend at her apartment, I agreed without hesitation. It rained until late Sunday and we made the most of it, spending what seemed like the entire weekend in her bedroom. Michelle finally had to go to work Sunday evening, and I returned to the hotel just after Sara, who was wandering around next door.

The image of her ashen features as she had watched Michelle and me that last Friday sprang to mind, and I knew we had to talk about it. We couldn't pretend it hadn't happened. I changed clothes and prowled around a while, mustering the courage to welcome her back. I approached the adjoining door and sheepishly placed my ear to one panel. Not a sound. I eased the door open and was surprised to find the door on her side already ajar, as if she'd been expecting me.

She was curled up on the bed, dressed casually in her favorite sweats. A novel rested in her lap and a pair of glasses was perched on her nose. She looked different somehow, and it took me a moment to notice that her dark hair, usually so perfectly coifed, was windblown and disheveled. She wore no makeup; I'd only seen her without but once before. She looked squeaky-clean. Young. Innocent. The sight was endearing. I watched her fondly, my heart warming.

"Welcome back," I greeted her quietly.

Emerald eyes lifted, peering over the top of her lenses. She didn't jump to remove them, as I'd expected. Her smile was hesitant as she raised her head and slowly reached up to remove the spectacles.

"Hi. I didn't think you were here." Her eyes narrowed. "Are you alone?"

I nodded. "Michelle's at work. Can I come in?"

"Of course."

I stepped inside and settled in one of the two arm chairs while she placed a bookmark between two pages and set her book on the nightstand.

"How was your weekend?" She asked the question first.

"Very nice. Very," I searched for the right word, "enlightening. And yours?"

She chuckled softly. I knew her mind was in the

gutter. "Not nearly so nice as yours, I'm sure. But somewhat enlightening. I think we need to talk," she sighed. "I need to apologize."

"Sara, it's —" She held up a hand to stop me.

"No really, I do. I need to get this out and over with so I can move on. I spent the whole weekend obsessing about it." Her features took on a look that was akin to shame. She was still upset. Her voice was missing its usual lilt, her words sounding almost terse and clipped. "This isn't easy for me to tell you, so I'm just going to spit it out." Her tongue quickly passed over her lips. "When I saw you — the two of you. I guess I was..." She looked at me, eyes wide with embarrassment and disbelief. "Jealous." She shook her head, trying to comprehend. "That's the only word I can come up with to describe it."

I was careful not to move, not to show any reaction as she continued.

"I know that sounds ridiculous. It *is* ridiculous. I've gotten so used to having you all to myself that I forget you have other people in your life. Other friends. Lovers." She was rambling, angrily berating herself, no longer looking at me. "It's so stupid. I can't believe I reacted that way. I can't believe I acted so stupid and that I have to apologize to you again. I don't want to keep doing things that I end up apologizing for. I'm so mad at myself."

Her tirade was becoming painful, even for me. "Sara, it's okay."

"I'm sorry."

"Sara." The name came out more sternly than I'd intended. "Enough. Stop it. You're forgiven. It's okay." The cloud lifted from her eyes as she focused on me, finally seeing me. She was thankfully quiet. "Look," I managed a lame smile. "I feel the same way. It's like I'm constantly worried that I'm going to say or do something that will put you off. I want to trust you, but I don't know how to do it. I don't know how to be close to a woman who isn't gay. Not really. It's foreign to me. I feel like I'm on eggshells all the time. Like one day you're going to see that we really have nothing in common and you'll just turn away."

"That's my fault. I shouldn't have turned my back on you before."

"No." I waved her off. "It isn't all about you. It's about others too. And about me. I worry too much about what people will think. I worry too much about losing people."

Silence stretched. I hadn't intended to say so much. I was brooding already, wishing I could take the words back.

"And you don't want to lose me." It was a statement.

I looked at her sheepishly. "No. I don't want to lose you."

Her smile reached her eyes. "I don't want to lose you either." She sighed again, relieved. "Why is this so difficult?"

I shrugged. "Unfamiliar territory. You're straight and I'm gay. And as much as I like to think that it doesn't make us that different, it does. We see the world differently."

"You make it sound hopeless."

"I didn't mean to," I admitted. "I'm overanalyzing and making it sound worse than it really is. It's just the mood I'm in."

"Maybe we're both worrying too much," she offered.

"Should I apologize?"

"Don't you dare." She laughed now, jumping from the bed and squatting down in front of the wet bar to offer me a Coke. "Are we done?"

"With this conversation? I think so." I took the can from her outstretched hand and popped the top open.

"Good." She settled back down on the bed, tucking her legs beneath her. "So tell me about your weekend."

I quickly checked her expression, not finding the smirk that I'd expected. "It rained most of the weekend, so we didn't get out much. We stayed at Michelle's apartment."

"Sounds like this might be getting serious." I knew she was fishing, and I smiled ironically.

"Funny that you should say that."

Her jaw dropped just a bit, her brows coming together. "You're going to move down here to be with her, aren't you."

Where could she possibly have gotten an idea like that?

"No. Definitely not."

Her brow smoothed over and she settled back again, waiting for me to continue.

"Michelle really has no intention of settling down right now."

"Have you?"

"Not with Michelle." I faced her squarely, my head tilting back. "Don't get me wrong," I began, feeling the need to explain. "Michelle's a sweet woman, and she's been good for me. Probably the best thing that could have happened to me right now. But we aren't a good fit. Know what I mean?" I wrinkled my nose as a picture of Michelle entered my mind, head tipped back, throaty laughter bursting from her lips. "She's a doll, though." I left my reverie and focused again on Sara, who was watching me closely. I grinned a little. "I know you're dying to ask, so I'll save you the trouble. Yes. She's an incredible lover."

Sara didn't wince at my words. Her smile was almost naughty. "I'm not a bit surprised." She stared at me for a few moments, making me wish I could read her thoughts. "You're not going to break her heart or anything, are you?"

"Oh, no." I shook my head and took a sip of my soda. "Actually, we talked about it." I regarded Sara carefully. "This isn't her first fling."

She laughed. "Is she yours?"

My face colored. "I guess you could say so. I've never gotten involved with anyone so quickly before. That's part of what I learned this weekend." She screwed up her face a bit, not following me. "That I can just enjoy Michelle without trying to marry her. I've never really been able to do that before."

"You mean you don't sleep around?" she laughed.

I was horrified. "Absolutely not."

"It's not true, then?" she asked, barely able to suppress the sudden twinkle in her eyes.

"What's not true?" I sensed a joke was coming.

"That lesbians are nymphomaniacs."

I laughed. "Just a myth, I'm afraid. Although my friend Susan might qualify."

She laughed loudly, then was silent when it occurred to me that once again, the conversation was focused on me.

"Enough about me. What's going on with you? How's everything with James? Are you still seeing him?"

She shook her head. "No. We split up a while ago."

"I'm sorry," I lied.

"I'm not. He wasn't good for me."

I digested this. "And it's hard to meet guys down here when Billy and I are your only friends."

"Don't worry. I'm in no rush to meet anybody." She brushed the comment aside. "Besides, we were talking about you."

"Yeah, well, I'm onto you now. You've been getting me to talk about myself nonstop lately, and you've barely said a word about yourself. This trust thing is supposed to go two ways."

She looked like the proverbial cat that swallowed the canary. "You figured me out, huh?" She uncurled her legs and stretched out on the bed, fluffing her pillows. "Okay, shoot. What do you want to know?"

The door was wide open, and I stepped in with both feet. "I want to know about your best friend in high school."

She flinched. "Right for the jugular." She swallowed hard and ran a hand through her hair. "I've never told this to anyone before."

I just watched her, expectantly, letting her take her time.

She took a deep breath to steady herself. "Her name was Tracy," she began. "We were best friends all through high school, and we did everything together." Her eyes wandered until they focused on the wall just above my head. "We always used to sleep over at each other's house. One night, Tracy was staying at my place. It was late and we were in bed, talking about boys. Out of nowhere she started telling me that she didn't understand why girls couldn't date other girls and that she liked me more than she'd ever liked any guy." She paused, her face looking pinched. "I don't really remember what happened after that. Except that she kissed me." She sneaked a look at me, monitoring my reaction.

Under other circumstances, I might have teased her. But she looked so stricken that I couldn't. I watched her, keeping my expression carefully closed, waiting for her to continue.

She dropped her eyes to her lap, unable to look at me any longer. "You're going to hate me for this." Her voice was so quiet I had to strain to hear her. "I just flipped out. I called her all kinds of names. I was so cruel. I told all the kids at school that she'd kissed me. Everybody made fun of her." Her voice was cracking as she finished. "I completely humiliated her."

My heart sank to the very pit of my stomach. I was speechless. Tortured eyes turned to me, gauging my reaction, asking for understanding, pleading for forgiveness. But I was powerless to hide my horror and repulsion. *Every young lesbian's worst nightmare.* I was so astonished and overwhelmed with grief for the young girl that Sara must have destroyed. My mind was screaming. *How could you do such a thing?*

Silence stretched as I fought my hostility. Her eyes registered my rejection, and she dropped her head, tears welling and flowing down her cheeks.

My response was hurting her, and I struggled with wanting to comfort her while still recoiling in anger and dismay. I fought to calm myself, knowing I had to forget my personal reaction and try to help her. I thought about how Sara must have felt all those years, knowing what she'd done. How she must have felt when I told her the truth about myself all those months ago. I knew in my heart that the Sara I had come to know must hate herself for what she'd done. To both of us. But what could I do? I could never give her the absolution she needed. She would have to find that for herself.

So much more had been going on with her all along. It hadn't occurred to me that there might be more to her rejection than I'd thought. My heart went out to her. I stood up, covering the distance between us in a few easy steps.

I settled down on the bed beside and just in front of her, swallowed my pride, and reached out to wrap my arms around her, pulling her close and rocking her as the tears poured in earnest.

"Don't hate me," she choked. She held me so tightly, burrowing her face in my neck as each sob racked her body.

"Shh. It's all right. I don't hate you. It's okay." I did my best to comfort her, holding her safely and letting my hand stroke the curls that fell forward on her brow. Whispering quietly. Telling her it had happened such a long time ago. That it was time for her to forgive herself. Time to let it go. I was completely immersed in her grief, closing my eyes and feeling my walls just crumble away. She hurt so much. I wanted to soothe her and take away all the pain. My face nuzzled in her hair as I dropped light, comforting kisses on her head. "Shh. It's okay." Over and over, I repeated the words. Holding her, my fingers combing through hair.

The shudders finally subsided; her breathing became even. She continued to cling to me, unmoving. A heavy sigh escaped her, and my eyelids squeezed together as I sighed in return. We'd made it. We'd gotten through it. My anger was nonexistent as my focus shifted. I was suddenly aware of whom my arms were wrapped around. I couldn't help thinking how good it felt as I inhaled deeply, savoring the clean outdoor smell of the hair that tickled my nose. She continued to hold me, and my lips curled in an involuntary smile.

The moment was fleeting, and I could only allow myself to admit how much I cared for that brief instant. I wished for another place and time. One where I could tell her how I felt without the inevitable rebuff. I kept my thoughts inside, holding them, cherishing them before finally letting them go, as if they'd never been.

With a quick squeeze I drew back, releasing both her and the fantasy. She was sniffing, rubbing her face on the sleeve of her sweatshirt.

"I'm such a shit," she muttered.

I chuckled softly to let her know I didn't agree. "Maybe you were a shit. You're not anymore. Kids are cruel when they're that age." My neck felt cool and empty where her face had just burrowed. I leaned back a little more, dropping one arm to the bed to prop myself up. My other hand rested on her shoulder, continuing to rub slowly.

"Sure. Look what I did to you. That was just this year." She still hadn't looked at me.

"We're past all that, remember?" She looked pitiful, her face all red and puffy. My thoughts drifted back to Tracy. "Did you ever get the chance to apologize to her?"

"No." She shook her head, staring past me blankly. "I think she still lives somewhere in Boston, though. But even if I could find her, I wouldn't know how to make it up to her. How to explain."

"Maybe you could just say that you're sorry. Sometimes that's enough." My brow furrowed as I contemplated her glassy look. "Do you have any idea why you reacted that way? Why you told all those other kids?"

"Oh, yeah. I know." She wiped the back of her hand across her face and sighed. "I did it because that kiss made my stomach flutter like nothing I'd ever felt before. I liked it, and it scared the hell out of me. I wanted to make sure it never happened again." She lifted her head now, turning swollen, bloodshot eyes to mine. "Care to analyze that, Leslie?"

Revelations were dropping by the minute. I was caught completely unprepared again. "Adolescent callowness."

She lifted a brow. "Think so?" I wasn't sure if her tone was hopeful or doubtful.

"Sure." I shrugged casually. "You reacted that way because you knew that the kiss was somehow taboo. It intrigued you, and it scared you at the same time." I didn't believe a word of what I was saying.

I searched her eyes, trying to read her thoughts. She wasn't meeting my gaze; she was staring at my mouth. "So, if you kissed me right now, it wouldn't feel the same way, right?" Her eyes fluttered and met mine.

My heart flip-flopped. My mind was racing. I didn't trust what I was hearing. *She's asking me to kiss her, right?* A rushing sound flooded my ears, and I had to remind myself to breathe. I searched her face, just inches away, for an answer. Her green eyes, made bright from the recent tears, were clear and completely focused on mine. Void of makeup to cover them, her tiny freckles winked at me. So unlike the image of the carefully put-together businesswoman that I always associated with her. So clean. So clear. So soft. My eyes wandered over her high cheekbones, down to her small pointed chin, then dropped to her long neck, and the pulse that was beating at the hollow of her throat. Back to her eyes. Still watching me. Waiting. Not backing down. Beckoning. Those lips. Made fuller, almost puffy from the crying. Slightly parted. How often I'd thought of those lips. I fashioned myself a thief as I imagined leaning in and stealing a kiss from that mouth. Could she know what she was asking? How could I ever find my way back to the safe place I'd found once I'd kissed those lips?

She tipped her head back, ever so slightly. I blinked, catching my breath, and leaned forward. Our eyes locked. Leaning closer. Closer. Her lashes fluttered down, lids now exposed. My heart was thumping. And my lips touched hers. Lightly. So lightly. Like a feather of innocence. I could taste the salt from her recent tears as I waited for her to pull away. But she didn't. Closer still. Was it her heartbeat or mine that I heard? Softly pressing, lingering. So warm. So yielding. No longer just touching, but parting. So gently. Her mouth opened, ever so slightly. Soft tongue. Tentative. Finding mine. Brief touch. Unmoving. So soft. So wet. It was too perfect. Too nice.

I was the one who ended the kiss. I brushed her lips again. Just one last time before I raised my head. My eyelids were heavy when I lifted them. I'd never seen her eyes so wide as they bore into mine, unflinching. I leaned back a little more to steady myself and catch my breath. Her lips were still parted, wet from the kiss. From my kiss. My heart was in my stomach, and my mind scrambled to gain control.

"I'm sorry," I stammered. "I shouldn't have —"

"Don't apologize. I asked you to kiss me." Her voice was as unwavering as her eyes, not giving away a hint of what she was thinking or feeling.

I was suddenly desperate to break the spell I was under and rid myself of the panic that threatened. I pulled my hand from her shoulder and placed it on the bed beside me, hoping that she couldn't see that I was shaking. Now I was the one who couldn't meet her eyes.

"I think," she was saying, "that you just shot a big hole through your own theory." She reached out and tugged the sleeve of my shirt. "So much for teenage innocence." Her tone became light. "What do you call that little flutter when you're twenty-eight years old?"

If she was playing with me, I wanted no part of it. "I think you're going to have to figure out that one on your own." I didn't mean to sound curt, but I know I did.

"Hey." She wrapped her fingers around my upper arm. "I hope you're not upset or anything. You don't have to worry. I'm okay. I'm not going to do anything crazy or anything. Really."

I realized that she thought I was worried about her reaction, when all I cared about was making sure she couldn't read my mind. Surely my heart was plainly on my sleeve.

I let my eyes move to hers and was surprised to see that she was smiling, looking almost exuberant. My feelings were safe. "You mean you're not going to hold it against me?"

"Nope." Her fingertip traced a cross over her heart. "I'm fine."

"Good." Great. Sara was fine. I had to escape, to give myself time to get a grasp on my raging emotions. But I could think of no way to get away easily. "Don't take this the wrong way or anything, but I need to go back to my room. Okay?"

Her smile fell. "Leslie. What's wrong?"

"Nothing. Really," I insisted.

"Are you upset?"

"I'm not upset. Sara. Really," I lied, now dangerously close to tears. Forcing a smile, I met her doubtful gaze. "I'm just tired. It's been a long weekend." Michelle seemed miles away. "And this conversation's been a little draining. That's all. Don't worry." I said the last words as I hoisted myself from the mattress. "Feel like taking a swim in the morning?"

"Sure." Her response was terse. "Knock when you're ready."

"Okay." Again I forced a smile. "Good night, Sara."

I wasn't sure if she replied. I turned blindly and made my way through the open doors, closing the one on my side and fumbling to lock it with shaking hands.

Chapter 11

I don't think I slept at all that night. My mind raced while I lay awake, replaying the events of the evening over and over, always lingering over the kiss. Then I mentally dragged myself back to reality and my anger took over. It had taken me so long to get over that infatuation. And now there I was, right back to where I'd been months ago. Old feelings swelled inside me.

Why had she wanted me to kiss her? Probably an experiment. A way to exorcise the past and the pain she'd suffered since high school. *Well, I hope it worked*. But what if she wanted more? What if she became curious and decided she wanted to explore her sexuality? Like Julie had. My thoughts drifted to Julie. That's all I had been to her. A curiosity. An experiment. Well, I wouldn't let it happen again. I'd learned that lesson long ago. And I would never, ever let myself be some kind of guinea pig for Sara.

By the time my alarm clock went off, I was bleary-eyed. Thankfully, the day passed without Sara mentioning what had happened the night before. Perhaps I'd imagined its significance.

The project was moving along quickly. Billy was ecstatic since it looked like we would meet all our original deadlines. My emotions were mixed. It would be good to get back home, but I'd grown fond of Atlanta as well.

Sara and I continued to spend much time together as always. I kept waiting for her to drop a bomb in my lap, but she didn't. Apparently she wanted to forget the kiss had ever happened, I reasoned. Either that, or the kiss had really been far more important to me than to her. I was probably right on both counts.

As the end of the week neared, Michelle called and invited both of us out to dinner on Thursday night. I fully expected Sara to turn down the invitation, but she accepted eagerly.

We took our rental car to a barbecue restaurant just outside Atlanta. The ribs were absolutely heavenly, and we made gluttons of ourselves. I'd been concerned that the evening might prove uncomfortable, but I needn't have worried. Michelle and Sara got along famously, and I found myself in the position of being a spectator, watching and laughing at their conversation, but not really participating. They were both in rare form, incredibly funny and boisterous.

My eyes moved between them, and I couldn't suppress the smile that came to my lips. They were so different, yet each so striking in her own way. Michelle so alluring, and Sara so lovely. My mind created an image of the two of them together, as lovers. They would make a great couple. *Oh, the heads would turn!* As the thought took hold, my stomach began to sour. *Great. I can see it now. I introduce them to each other, and they fall in love.* I shook my head and spent the rest of dinner trying not to let the thought slip back into my mind.

When we returned to the hotel, Sara joined Michelle and me in my room. They continued to banter for a short while before Michelle had to leave.

"I have a lesson at six," she grumbled. She turned to me and asked if I was going to stay in town for the weekend.

"I'm not sure," I told her. "I was thinking I should probably go home."

She frowned playfully. "I can't convince you to stay?"

I was aware of Sara's watchful eyes. "I'll think about it and call tomorrow, okay?"

Satisfied, she turned back to Sara and said good-bye. Sara responded by thanking her and telling her that she'd had fun. Awkwardly, I followed Michelle to the door, expecting to drop a quick kiss on her lips before I let her escape. But she caught me up in her arms, kissing me slow and hard until I was out of breath.

"I really think you should stay," she said under

her breath. Then she grinned and put a hand to my cheek before vanishing behind the door. My cheeks were flushed when I turned back to Sara's reproaching eyes.

"You didn't kiss me like that."

My head snapped back. My neck was suddenly taut with anxiety as the emotions I had so carefully suppressed all week burst forth, exploding in anger.

"I'm not sleeping with you, either." The razor-sharp words stung her, betraying my feelings. We stared at each other, both of us surprised and fuming. I became contrite, wanting to apologize but not trusting myself to speak.

Her eyes narrowed. "Christ. Where in the hell did that come from? What's going on with you?"

"Nothing is going on with me." I moved to the bed and flung myself across it. "Stop analyzing me." I was acting like a spoiled brat.

She continued to watch me, frowning. "Are you mad because I didn't leave you two alone? Because I went to dinner with you?"

My laugh was brittle. "Yeah. That's it, Sara. You're right again. You know me so well." Sarcasm dripped from my voice.

"I don't think I know you at all." Her voice was quiet, almost sad. She strolled to the door, slowly pulling it open and stepping out to the hallway. I fought the urge to call her back, my eyes burning as I heard the lock click into place behind her.

The downward spiral had begun. I was self-destructing and sabotaging the friendship. I could see it, feel it, and know that I was responsible. But I didn't know how to stop it. How would I ever get past this? How could I ever get back to just being her friend?

Sara joined me for breakfast the next morning. We were quiet and tentative with each other, both still stinging from the night before. The day wore slowly, and I was still undecided about whether or not to go home. I thought of the questions that Susan would ask. And the answers that I didn't have for her. Maybe I'd just stay in Atlanta after all.

At the end of the day I looked around half-heartedly for Sara, not surprised when I couldn't find her. Assuming she'd already left for the hotel, I trudged back on my own. Once there, I called Michelle to let her know I'd decided to stay in town. She explained that she had to work that night at the bar, but maybe I could come down later and keep her company? I agreed that I would, then changed into shorts and a T-shirt while I tried to relax and watch the evening news.

A light tapping from the other side of the connecting doors interrupted my thoughts. Reluctantly, I swung my legs off the bed and stepped to the door, pulling it open. Sara was leaning against the doorjamb, dressed in jeans and a hunter green sweater, a jacket and overnight bag slung over one shoulder. Her expression was almost sheepish.

"Hi." Her eyes dropped, taking in my casual attire. "I thought maybe we could share a cab to the airport."

I shook my head, feeling like a jerk again. "I decided to stay."

She looked crestfallen. "Michelle?"

I nodded. "She's working tonight, but I'll probably go down to the bar and join her later."

Again she nodded quietly, then smiled weakly. "I had a lot of fun with her last night. I can see why you're so attracted to her."

"She's a sweetie," I agreed.

"But it's not serious." She was fishing again, and I had to laugh.

"No. It's not serious."

She nodded again, hedging, looking like she wanted to say something else. "I was hoping that we could talk on the plane. I had something I wanted to tell you."

"Not another confession."

She smiled. "Well, kind of."

My heart sank. I didn't think I could take much more. "Should I sit down?" I tried my best to be lighthearted.

She nodded, then reached out to touch my arm as I turned away. "No. I was just kidding."

Relieved, I leaned against the door, careful to keep distance between us.

"I think you've misread me." She stopped and laughed at herself. "I mean, I'm sure I've been difficult to read."

I decided to sit down after all, pulling out a chair several feet away and folding myself into it. She remained where she was, leaning against the doorway.

"I've wanted to tell you," her face colored as she paused. "The other night, when you kissed me . . ." I tried not to flinch as I braced myself for her words. "It was very nice. I wanted you to know that it was special."

I felt my resolve weaken as I returned her steady gaze.

"And last night. I wasn't trying to be a jerk when I said that about you kissing Michelle." She took a deep breath, pressing farther into the doorway. "I was jealous. Pure and simple. I wanted to kiss you that way too."

After a solid week of preparing myself for the possibility of this moment, my response was well rehearsed, quick, and cutting. "Ah. The old curiosity and the straight-woman theory comes through again."

She looked like I'd kicked her in the stomach.

"That's all you can say? I tell you how I feel and you throw it back in my face?"

In all of my imaginings, I'd never anticipated how I might reply to her anger. Or her hurt. *Stop it. Stop it.* "I'm sorry. That wasn't fair," I backpedaled. "This just feels vaguely familiar, and, you know, rule number one."

"Fuck your rules. I can't believe I bothered to tell you this." Her hands were clenching and unclenching, her face bright red. "God. I'm so stupid."

"Sara." I stood up and moved toward her. "I'm being a jerk."

"You're right. You are." She began to back away from me, shaking her head.

Oh god, I'd done it again. "Sara." Again I approached, but she continued to back away until she was in her own room and it was I who was standing in the doorway.

She turned back to face me just as she reached the door to the hallway. "Tell me. If you're not serious about Michelle, then what's the attraction? What is it, Leslie? Why are you seeing her? Is it the excitement?" She was goading me. "Just for fun? Great sex? What?" Her hand was resting on the doorknob behind her. "Or is it just your ego?"

"It's safe," I shrugged.

"Because it's safe? That's sad." She shook her head, her tone sarcastic. "That's really sad. But you know, I'm not a bit surprised." Her laugh was caustic. "I have a plane to catch." Before I could think of a retort, the door was open and she was gone.

Chapter 12

I paced the room for what seemed like hours until I could no longer stand it. I slipped into a pair of jeans and sneakers, pulled a sweater over my head, and grabbed the keys to the rental car. Without so much as a look in the mirror, I was out the door and headed for the bar.

Once in the car, I changed my mind and headed for the highway, feeling the need to clear my mind before I saw Michelle. I scolded myself over and over. How could I have talked to Sara like that? How could I have been so vicious, so vindictive? *Congratulations, Leslie. Job well done.*

The knot in my stomach took hold and grew, overwhelming me until I felt ill. My instincts told me to track her down, call her, anything. Let her know I'd do anything to take it back. But the other part of me took over, working to calm me down, coldly pointing out that it was better this way.

I tried to convince myself that it didn't matter, all the while knowing that nothing else did. Finally, some two hours later, I found my way back to town and the place where I knew I could find some solace.

Thankfully, Michelle was glad to see me. I found her in the room with the dance floor, standing at the far end behind the bar, her chin propped on an upturned hand as she watched several couples dancing. The smile on her face disappeared once she registered my distress. She moved to my side of the bar to wrap her arms around me in a comforting hug.

"Honey, you look absolutely miserable," she whispered in my ear. My chin trembled, and I felt dangerously close to tears. She stood back to search my eyes. "What's wrong, Leslie?"

I couldn't speak. I was too afraid the tears would spill. She hugged me again, holding me a little longer before pulling back and guiding me to a bar stool.

"Sit," she directed, and I complied. Miserably, I just stared at her while she held my hand and watched me.

"Is this about Sara?"

I was astonished. "How did you know?" I found my voice.

"She was here," she said quietly.

"She was here?" Incredulous, I nearly jumped from my seat, but Michelle reached out to hold me still.

She nodded. "Don't be mad. She needed someone to talk to and I was the only one she could think of."

"She came here to talk to you?" My spine stiffened with fury, then swiftly changed to anxiety. "What did she say?"

Michelle shrugged. "That you had argued. That she was on her way to the airport but couldn't leave." Her smile was lopsided. "Do you want to tell me about it?"

"No." I rolled my eyes. "Yes. I think I need to." I sighed. "Do you mind?"

"That's what I'm here for," she assured me. "Hang on, I'll get you a drink." She slipped back to the other side of the bar and returned with a glass of chablis and a bowl of pretzels.

I munched hungrily on the pretzels, remembering that I hadn't bothered with dinner. "She actually came in here alone?" I couldn't believe it.

"Yep. She sat right there." She pointed to the stool next to mine. "We had a good talk, actually. I like her."

I dropped my voice, unreasonably distrustful. "What do you mean, you like her."

She flashed me a dirty look. "Don't be paranoid." She planted a pretzel in my mouth. "She cares about you."

"Sure she does." I was sarcastic. "Did she tell you what I said to her?"

Michelle leaned forward on her elbows. "Why don't you tell me what happened."

137

Gratefully, I poured out the whole story in detail. From the day I'd first met Sara up until earlier that night. Michelle was careful not to interrupt, letting me rant and rave until I fully exhausted myself and finished the story. Her smile was sweet and reassuring when I finished. She didn't look at all surprised by anything I'd said.

"I think you should be honest with her, Leslie. Give her a chance."

I looked at her closely, really seeing her for the first time that night. "Thanks for listening. It wasn't very fair of me to dump all of this on you."

She leaned over a little closer, her smile sincere. "It's okay. You know that." She held my hand. "I hate to see you so unhappy." She tilted her head back, and her eyes focused on a spot above my head. She grinned mischievously, and I couldn't figure out why until I felt a pair of hands drop lightly down on my shoulders.

I jumped, knowing that it was Sara who held me firmly in place. "Why do I feel like I've been ambushed?" I directed the question to Michelle. "Traitor."

Michelle squeezed my hand before laughing innocently and holding up both hands. "Hey. I just work here." She inclined her head toward Sara. "Have a seat. I have customers to serve." She disappeared to the other end of the bar, and I was left staring straight ahead, trying to look fascinated by the bottles of liquor that lined the wall. *Trapped.*

I could feel Sara's hesitation as she lifted her hands and settled into the stool beside me. She dropped several bills on the counter before swiveling to face me, her knees pressing against my thigh. I tried not to pull away, and she didn't bother to move them.

I sipped my wine while I steadied myself. "I thought you were going back to Boston," I said as quietly as I could above the music.

"This is where I want to be." She tapped the counter, then let her hands fall to her lap. My fingers wrapped around my glass, and I turned my head so I could face her squarely.

"I'm glad you're here. That you decided to stay." I swallowed my pride, thankful for the opportunity to try to make things right. "I didn't mean what I said back at the hotel. I wish I could take it all back." I shook my head, unable to explain myself, unable to be completely honest. I focused on my drink, sipping it slowly before turning back to her cautiously. "Why did you stay?"

She chose her words carefully. "On my way to the airport, I thought about what you'd said. The part about being involved with Michelle because it was safe." She paused before continuing. "It struck me that I've been doing just that for most of my life. Playing it safe, that is." She smiled wryly. "Then I thought about the way you jumped down my throat when I told you that I was jealous of that kiss. Is it possible that maybe you were just trying to push me away?" She watched my reaction carefully. "Am I close?"

"Closer than I'd probably like to admit," I mumbled.

She grinned at my words. "I've gone about this all wrong. I've been teasing you and trying to get your attention in all the wrong ways." I looked away, and she touched my knee, prompting me to look at her, to listen to what she was saying. "Especially after you told me about Julie. I should have known that you would be defensive."

I took another sip and averted my eyes. This time she touched my hand, her fingertips lingering over my wrist. She dipped her head down a bit, her eyes completely focused on mine. Dark. Serious. Riveting. She drew her hand away, slowly, content that she had my full attention. Even in the darkness of the room, I could see her nervousness.

"I should never have played with you like that. But I didn't know how to tell you." Her mouth had difficulty forming the words; her lips twitched ever so slightly as she forced herself to go on. "I have feelings for you, Leslie. Feelings that I don't know what to do with."

My eyes squinted as I felt her fear. I opened my mouth to say something, but she rushed on. "I've been hoping that you might feel the same way. That's why I came here tonight. To find out. If you don't feel anything, you can tell me. Just please don't be nasty about it, okay?"

Relief swept through me, fear gave way to hope, and hope became a slow warmth uncurling inside of me. I watched her skeptically, not trusting my ears. I recognized the stress around her eyes, the tension that was pulling at the corners of her mouth as she braced herself for my reply.

"It's not just you." I swallowed hard, feeling the need to speak cautiously. "I've been fighting feelings for you for a long time." I watched as the heavy burden was lifted from her shoulders. Her features began to relax.

"You have?"

I nodded, feeling inadequate, not knowing what to say. I closed my eyes. "I'm not very good at this. It isn't easy for me."

She leaned in closer, so that her breath was on my cheek. "What makes you think this is so easy for me?" The words got through to me.

"You don't do this every day?" It was my turn to smile wryly.

"Not if I can help it." She sipped her wine, and we were silent, neither of us knowing where to begin. "The question is, what do we do about it?"

"Actually, I decided a long time ago not to do anything about it."

Her eyes grew dark. "Is that what you still want to do?"

A sudden chill claimed my spine as I entertained the notion of lying. It wasn't too late. I could still get out. "No." The word burst from my throat before I could catch it. "That's not what I want."

A smile sneaked into those eyes. "Good. I don't either." She looked relieved and hesitant all at once.

I was silent as we sipped our wine, taking the opportunity to digest her words, internalizing that everything had changed. And yet nothing had. It was a start, an open door. I decided to push aside the doubts that I knew would come. They could wait.

"So what do we do now?" My nerves were frazzled.

She reached out and wrapped a hand around my wrist. "We dance."

"Are you kidding?" I pulled away involuntarily.

She laughed and tugged on my arm. "I'm serious. Come on. This is the only song I've known all night."

I listened for a moment, recognizing Donna Summer's voice, and I was instantly aghast. "I can't dance with you to 'Love to Love You, Baby.'" Again I pulled back, which only made her laugh harder.

"Yes, you can." She stood up, encouraging me to follow. My eyes flew to Michelle, begging her to come to my rescue. But she was chatting with one of the waiters, oblivious to my predicament.

With a groan, I let Sara lead me through the maze of tables and out on the dance floor. She didn't release my wrist until we were surrounded by other couples. I avoided her gaze as my eyes fell from couple to couple, noting how bodies were pressing against other bodies. Panic rose in my throat, and my feet were rooted to the floor.

"I can't dance to this song," I called above the music. She stepped to one side and I followed as the song began blessedly fading out.

"You're in luck," she laughed. I prayed silently for a faster song that I might know, one that I could get lost in and lose my self-consciousness. I strained to catch the first bars of the next song, my heart sinking when I recognized the beginning of a soft, sultry love song.

My eyes flew to hers. "Should we sit down?"

She laughed and tugged on the sleeve of my sweater. "No. I want to dance."

"To this?" Other couples began to wrap their arms about each other, their bodies coming together.

"Relax. I don't bite." She was smiling as she held out both hands. Hesitating, I looked from the outstretched hands to her face, searching her eyes, not believing what was happening. *Surely she'll pull the rug out from under me any moment.* Her smile began to falter, her brow furrowing with uncertainty.

The music swelled and a sigh escaped me as I leaned forward.

"You realize, of course, that this requires my touching you."

"I would hope so," she chuckled and held her hands out a little higher, waiting for me to meet them. I lifted leaden arms, finding her hands with mine, pausing to relish the small pleasure. The fingers of my right hand entwined her left. I stepped closer as our clasped hands came to rest behind her back, settling just below her waist. My other hand fell to her hip, her palm smoothing up my arm to rest on my shoulder. We began to move, slowly, awkwardly. I concentrated on the dancing, trying to find her rhythm.

"Is this okay?" Her voice was foreign, small, weak, unsure. I tilted my head back to search her eyes. No longer playful, they were talking to me, silently anxious, betraying her nervousness.

I forgot my own fears and squeezed the hand that rested in mine.

"It's okay," I said simply, softly, knowing that my expression probably told her far more than words. She relaxed with a heavy sigh. Her hand left my shoulder and dropped to wrap around my waist as she stepped closer, pressing her full length against mine. My entire body shuddered involuntarily, and I closed my eyes. Giving up, giving in. I put my arm around her back; my hand reached up to touch the curls at the nape of her neck. I turned my face in to her throat and breathed deeply, reveling in her scent, in the perfect fit of our bodies, pressed tightly and moving slowly.

It felt nice, holding her that way, twisting my fingers in her hair, moving dreamily, letting the music swell inside me. Wondering if she could possibly be feeling even a hint of the same.

Too soon the song ended, and the *thump, thump, thump* of a heavy bass obliterated the sweetness of what it had replaced. We stopped moving and embraced. We lingered, hugged, reluctantly released. We separated and stepped back, awkwardly appraising each other. I didn't mind that she wasn't smiling. Her long smoldering stare said enough. She swallowed hard, and I grinned tentatively, reaching for her hand. Without a word, I led her back through the throngs of people now on the dance floor and headed back to our bar stools.

Michelle was immediately in attendance, laughing and joking and quickly refilling drinks as a group of her friends gathered around us. I wondered if she was aware of what was going on between Sara and me. If she was, she didn't show it, except that perhaps she touched me less often and less intimately. I was at a loss for words with Sara, so I was grateful for the forced distraction of Michelle's friends. Sara didn't ask me to dance again, and in fact didn't talk to me much as we chatted with the others. But I was aware of the occasional hand that would drop on my arm, and the knee that resumed its pressure against my thigh.

It was nearly midnight when Sara leaned over, her breath on my neck as she whispered in my ear. "You know, I think I'm going to need a ride back to the hotel."

I regarded her closely for a moment. "That's right. You took a cab here, didn't you?"

She nodded. "I don't suppose I could catch a ride back with you?" Her dark head tipped to one side. "Unless that would spoil your plans for the evening?"

My heart jumped, my eyes flying to Michelle and then back to Sara. The whole situation felt so awkward. "I'm sure Michelle will understand," I said evenly. "Are you ready to go soon?"

"Ready when you are."

I nodded, definitely ready, and caught Michelle's hand as she wandered by. A moment of guilt touched me as I stammered. "I'm going to give Sara a ride back to the hotel," I told her.

She looked from me to Sara, then back again. I thought for a moment that she might ask to see me later, but she didn't. She just smiled and reached down to grab something, then ducked under the bar to join us on our side. She held Sara's overnight bag and jacket in one hand. I stood up to accept her bear hug, feeling awkward, knowing that it was a different kind of hug altogether from what I was used to getting from her. She squeezed me tight, holding on.

"I hope this works out for you," she whispered.

Sadness and confusion filled me. Things were moving too fast, too far out of control. "Whoa. Wait a minute —"

She silenced me with a quick kiss on the cheek. "We had an understanding, remember? It's okay. Call me." She gave me a meaningful stare and turned to Sara, placing the bag in one hand and grabbing up the other in both of hers.

"Thank you." Those were the only words I heard Sara say before Michelle gave her a hug as well. I watched Sara's face as Michelle hugged her and whispered something in her ear. My mind was reeling, not quite believing what was happening. I watched Sara nod as Michelle stepped back, and told myself that I would call Michelle tomorrow.

"I won't," was all Sara said.

Michelle turned and smiled, squeezing my arm as she dipped back down and under the bar. She waved briefly before turning back to her friends, and Sara and I began making our way to the exit.

Silence settled over us once we were outside. The gravel of the parking lot crunched beneath my sneakers as we walked side by side, our shoulders occasionally brushing.

My thoughts were still on Michelle. "What did Michelle say to you back there?" I asked as we reached the car.

She looked at me as I unlocked the passenger door. "I don't think I want to tell you that right now. Maybe later."

I said I understood, thinking that I probably didn't want to tell her what Michelle had said to me, either.

The radio blared to life when I started the engine, causing me to jump and quickly turn the noise off. "Sorry." I looked at her, chagrined. "I was in a foul mood driving here."

Sara turned in her seat, shyly reaching out and lifting my hand from the steering wheel. I watched her bring it to her lap and hold it, her head bent as she traced my palm with one finger.

"What kind of a mood are you in now?" she

asked, her voice low as she continued to follow her finger with her eyes.

I smiled at her attempted casualness. "Anxious. Cautious. Confused." The words dropped one by one as I sighed.

Her eyes touched mine. "Me too," she admitted, still stroking my hand. Silence stretched as I firmly pushed away the reproaching words that tried to fill my mind. She stared out through the windshield, and my eyes traced the outline of her profile. Dark curls falling on her brow. Strong narrow nose, perhaps too long to be perfect. Small chin, tipped up, turning toward me.

"Can I do just one thing before we go?" Her tongue slid across her upper lip, then the lower, before ducking back inside her mouth, making her nervousness transparent.

My heart thumped in my chest. I nodded, staring into her eyes, shutting out the voices in my mind. Her hand moved to my cheek, then up to my temple and into my hair. Her breathing became uneven.

I reached up and covered her hand with my own, guiding her hand down, across my cheek until the palm covered my lips. I kissed her hand before releasing it. My lips tingled as her palm withdrew. The tips of her fingers lightly traced the edges of my mouth before drifting gently across my lips, tracing the top and then the bottom. She leaned closer, her eyes intent on my mouth. Soft lips replaced fingertips.

My eyelids fluttered down and we stayed motionless, our lips barely meeting. Then her hand slid to my neck as she urged me closer. I complied, reaching both hands to the softness of her cheeks. Her fingers caressing my neck; the pressure of her lips deepened. My fingers moved to her temples, combing the curls back from her brow.

The quiet was broken by a soft whimper escaping her throat. She pulled me closer still. Her lips were no longer gentle. The softness had given way to urgency. Her lips parted; her head tilted to one side. Our mouths opened, and her soft tongue found mine. She kissed me hungrily, so thoroughly I couldn't breathe. An eternity passed, and I knew only that mouth, exploring eagerly, wanting mine.

I was light-headed by the time her mouth released me, her arms moving to encircle me as she tucked her face in my neck. I held her close, smoothing her hair, unable to resist the smile that crept to my lips as her hot breath tickled my neck. She was breathing heavily, her body almost shivering as she pressed against mine. We were quiet, holding each other for some time before she found her voice.

"You've been holding out on me," she sighed, her voice low and husky.

My smile grew and I chuckled.

She lifted her head, sitting up and leaning back until her face was inches from mine. Her lids were heavy, brows pulled together, as her eyes searched my face. Her head moved slowly from side to side.

"I had no idea." Her voice hinted at wonderment.

I continued to watch her. To love her.

"Are you okay?" My fingers were still entwined in the curls at her neck.

She read my meaning, a smile touching the dark eyes. "Yeah. I'm okay." Her face broke out in a grin.

"I'm very okay." She kissed me again, this time with short, quick kisses that nearly bruised my lips. She settled back in the car seat, her eyes still focused on mine. "Except that I can't get close enough to you, and my arm is falling asleep."

I jumped back a little, releasing the arm that I had trapped.

"Should we go then?" I asked.

She nodded, waiting for me to engage the gears before retrieving my hand and holding it firmly in hers. She didn't release it until we arrived at the hotel. I pulled the car up to the front lobby entrance and let the valet park it for us.

Sara stayed in her room only long enough to drop off her overnight bag and jacket. I took a moment to glance in the mirror, wishing I had spent more time primping earlier in the evening.

Sara's reflection hovered just above my right shoulder in the mirror, and our eyes met. I studied her face, searching for a sign that reality had sunk in, that she had come to her senses. She'd been away from me for less than a minute, and already the doubts were creeping in.

My expression must have given me away, because she raised a warning brow and smiled. Then she stepped closer, her arms around my waist urging me to lean back against her. My hands clasped hers and I sighed heavily, watching our reflection as her head tipped down until her lips were brushing my neck. Goose bumps rose along my arm. Her hand found them and rubbed them away, a satisfied chuckle in her throat. I shivered, and she met my eyes again.

She grinned. Beamed, really. Something between exuberance and precociousness. My eyes traveled over the image in the mirror. Her face glowing, so close to my own. Her arms around my waist. Our hands entwined. While my eyes studied that image, my mind rejected it. Surely this wasn't real.

"This feels a little weird," I confessed.

She sighed and gave me a quick squeeze. "I know. But I've thought about this so much that it's been real to me for a long time."

"Really?" Had she really thought of me this way? I couldn't comprehend it.

"Really," she said simply, her gaze focused on mine in the mirror. "Do you know," she moved her face closer so that our faces were side by side, "that you look absolutely petrified?"

I rolled my eyes, wishing I weren't so transparent. "Thank you. I am."

"Me too," she laughed nervously. "Downright scared, actually." I was touched by her sincerity as relief flooded me. "I want the chance to know you better. This way." Her words stumbled a bit. "You know. Dating."

"Dating?" I laughed at her choice of words, and her face blanched. I turned in the circle of her arms. My hands went to her shoulders, then behind her neck. "You want to date me?" I teased.

"Yeah. Is that the wrong word or something? Is there some special word or terminology that I'm supposed to be using?" Her face was completely red.

"No," I assured her, smiling. "Dating is fine. I just can't believe I'm hearing this from you."

"Believe it." Her eyes flashed green as her chin tipped defiantly.

"I'll try," I sobered. "I want to."

"Good." She kissed me lightly, without passion.

"We can go slowly," I said against her mouth.

"Slowly," she echoed. "I'm not going anywhere."

I hugged her tightly, and she squeezed me in return, chuckling in my ear. "You just can't kiss me like you did in the car — or I won't be responsible for my actions."

I laughed and released her. She leaned back and appraised me. "Could I stay with you tonight?"

I thought my heart would explode. She jumped to reassure me, placing her hands on my shoulders and squeezing quickly. "I'll behave. I promise. I don't want this to end." She faltered, looking embarrassed. "I want to wake up and know that this really happened."

"I would like you to stay very much," my voice sounded serious as I hugged her again. She withdrew from my arms, her smile playful again as she made her way back to her room.

"I'll go change," she said, disappearing behind the door.

In a fog, I readied myself for bed, fretting over what to wear. Finally, I slipped an oversize T-shirt over my head and nervously turned out the light and climbed into bed, listening to Sara scurrying around next door. Soon the light that shone from her room into mine was extinguished, and I could sense rather than see her presence beside my bed.

"Are you there?" asked her quiet voice.

"Right here." I reached up a hand and found hers, then lifted the covers back and scooted over to make room for her. Her weight settled into the mattress beside me as my eyes got used to the dark. Without speaking, she lay back, her head resting in the pillows. Again, my nerves got the better of me and I lay beside her, unmoving, until at last she spoke.

"Can I hold you?" The words were so quiet that I had to strain to hear them. My eyes closed, and a sigh escaped me. She was being so sweet. So cautious and careful. Again I felt the tugging at my heart.

Without a word, I slipped an arm beneath her shoulders, urging her closer as she curled her body against my side. Her face rested near my collarbone as she tucked an arm around me. My arm went to her back, slowly rubbing through the thin cotton of her T-shirt. She sighed heavily and slipped a leg over one of mine, snuggling closer.

"Good night, Les." She pressed her lips against my throat.

"Good night, Sara." I combed my fingers through her hair, letting my hand trail up and down her back as a smile curved on my lips. I stared up toward the ceiling, relishing the moment, thanking the gods for the gift they'd bestowed. The doubts could wait until tomorrow. All that mattered right now was the face tucked so neatly into my neck, the glowing heat that covered the entire length of my body, and the soft, steady breath that floated across my chest. I pressed my lips to her brow, and we curled into each other, closer still.

Chapter 13

My eyes flew open at six o'clock, and I found myself mentally taking a quick inventory of body parts. I was lying on my side. Sara was curled up against my back, fitting closely, one arm wrapped around my waist.

I strained my ears, searching for a sign of wakefulness. But her breathing was slow and even as she slept. I fought the need to sneak out and go to the bathroom, wanting instead to stay and luxuriate against her. Finally, physical need won out, and I carefully lifted her arm and extracted myself from her embrace. I tiptoed to the bathroom, brushed my teeth and foolishly tried to run a comb through my hair before returning to bed.

I approached the bed from her backside, noting that she hadn't moved an inch, and leaned over to peek at her face. Long lashes were lying against high cheekbones, and her lips were slightly parted as she continued to sleep soundlessly. I lifted the covers and carefully slipped in behind her, tentatively moving arms and legs until I was tucked in, the curves of my body fitting neatly against hers.

Sleep eluded me. My mind and body were alive with pleasure, with an overwhelming sense of fullness and wonder. All the apprehension I had felt the night before was nonexistent as I stared straight ahead, my eyes focusing on the dark hair curling off her slender neck, not quite meeting the neckline of her T-shirt. As I stared, that area of bare skin began calling to me. Teasing me.

My lips found the spot, brushing lightly, lingering. I breathed deeply, loving her scent, arousal already swelling inside me. My lips traveled up along her hairline, behind an ear, down the side of her neck, settling where her neck met her shoulder.

"Mmm." The sigh escaped her dreamily, and she pressed herself against me snugly. Smiling now, I reached up and tugged the neckline of her T-shirt down, pressing my lips there. Circling. Licking and nibbling gently.

She shifted back against me and I put my arm beneath her pillow, bending it down at the elbow so I could touch her hand. Her fingers moved and entwined with mine, squeezing gently.

My mouth continued its journey as my other hand

drifted to her shoulder and down her arm, softly tickling before wiggling under the sleeve and covering her bare shoulder. Then my fingers reached down, trailing the bare skin along her collarbone, finding the quickening heartbeat in her throat, sliding along her neck, over her chin. My mouth crept up near the top of her spine, and I lifted my eyes to peer over her shoulder, watching my fingers as they found her lips. Her eyes were still closed as she met each fingertip with its own kiss. Her lips parted slowly, and her tongue found a finger, pulling it inside her mouth, softly sucking before releasing it to find another. The full wetness of her mouth sent a tremor through my belly, shaking me thoroughly, making me weak. I caught the smile that was dancing on her lips as she squeezed the hand that rested in hers.

When I recovered, my mouth had claimed her neck, opening wide as my tongue teased her, teeth grazing her smooth skin. Her mouth released my fingers, and her free hand moved down and behind her until it was on my hip, rubbing slowly, then urging me closer.

My hand moved high across her chest, up and over the curve of her shoulder, finally released from the sleeve of her shirt. Then my hand traveled along her arm, moving down, pressing into her forearm, lingering over her wrist until my hand found and covered hers where it was pressing on my backside. The strength of her hand surprised me as she gripped my fingers.

My knee came up behind hers, pushing gently until her body shifted, her leg bending as her weight shifted forward. My body moved against her. Her hand turned and lifted mine, moving it to her hip as she urged me to touch her there.

Without conscious thought, my hand traveled the side of her thigh, feeling the hard muscles tensing as I kneaded her flesh. I reached down behind her knee, tickling her, feeling her body shiver as my hand moved up and forward, hesitating over the softness of her inner thigh. My breathing was heavy as I became fully aware of the reactions of her body. She was squirming, anticipating my touch, her hand urging mine closer.

I hesitated, fingers stretching along her skin as I resisted the temptation to explore further. My hand moved upward, across the cotton underwear that hugged her hip, under her shirt, slowing as it curled to caress the taut skin that stretched across her belly. Fingers dipped to tease along the elastic waistband. She stretched up both hands now, grasping the arm that cradled her head, causing me to bend a bit more, move my body even closer, as I wrapped myself around her.

My lips moved behind her ear, teasing, her body shivering in reply. My heart thumped as I focused on the smooth skin of her stomach, my fingers finding and tracing each rib along her rib cage. My hand moved upward, brushing the soft swell of her breasts. I held my breath as I hesitated, luxuriating in anticipation, feeling the sweetness of her body as she strained expectantly. My hand was between her small breasts, slowly circling as I teased her, prolonging the moment until my hand lightly covered a breast, the nipple straining against my palm.

A long moan escaped her, urging me on, causing me to lose any inhibitions that I might still have.

The pressure from my hand increased as I touched her, caressing her, holding the fullness of her small breast before finding her nipple again and rolling it between my fingers. She was moaning now, melting back into me, her body weak and languid. I gathered her in my arms, my hand moving between both breasts now, gently rubbing, pinching, delighting in the way her body arched against me.

She was squeezing my other hand tightly, her breathing ragged as she began to move in earnest.

"Leslie." My name burst from her lips, her voice low and throaty as she twisted her head back, lifting one hand to the back of my head as she claimed my mouth with hers. Her passion exploded with that kiss, and she slipped down against me, lying on her back while she urged me over her.

My body moved on top of hers, my hands falling to her breasts as my mouth found hers again. She held my tongue inside her mouth, sucking deeply as her arms bent around my neck, crushing me to her.

I pushed the fabric of her shirt away, and my mouth joined my hands as lips and tongue and fingers danced across her nipples, causing her to cry out again.

"Leslie." Again my name was on her lips, this time with such urgency that I lifted my head, suddenly uncertain. I found her eyes, wide open and staring into mine, silently screaming with desire.

"Are you okay?" I whispered breathlessly.

She bit her bottom lip. "Please. Don't stop." Her words melted me, and I buried my face in her breasts, kissing her sweetly as her fingers raked my scalp. One hand moved down as the other continued to caress her, my mouth insistent on her breast.

Fingers flitted across her belly, dipping inside the waistband of her underwear.

Unbidden emotions rose inside me, making me shiver with a sudden rush of nervousness. I hesitated, faltered. Other images rushed to my mind. *What am I doing?* my inner voice screamed. *This is Sara. Sara.* Shaking now, I relaxed against her, my head dropping down to rest on her chest, my arms growing weak and limp as I lay unmoving, breathing hard. *Sara.*

Her body stilled beneath me, the heartbeat under my ear growing steady. Her hands relaxed in my hair, becoming gentle as she brushed my forehead. Then her hands were sure and strong, rubbing my back, easing the tension in my shoulders.

"Come here." She spoke quietly, lifting herself just enough to reach down and urge me forward. Without meeting her gaze, I buried my face in her neck, completely embarrassed, feeling a failure. *How could I have let this happen?*

Her hands moved up and down my back, slowly comforting and caressing. They found their way beneath my shirt, her fingers cool against the heat of my skin. I sighed heavily, trying to clear my mind, trying to feel nothing but the luxury of her hands on my body.

The pressure from her hands increased, her breathing becoming uneven again as she moved beneath me, lifting me so that her hands could move to my side. She tugged at my shirt, pulling it up and over my head so quickly that I hardly noticed. Gentle kisses dropped on my neck, my cheek, across my eyelids. Hands were everywhere, exploring my bare skin, lifting me. Fingers shyly brushed across my breasts.

My body shuddered, arousal rekindled, and I raised myself on one elbow. My mouth touched hers and I kissed her deeply as my hand found her breasts, teasing her nipples until she was moaning again. She repeated my name, asking me not to stop.

My heart swelled, and I gathered her close, still kissing her as my hand journeyed across her belly once again. She held me tightly as my fingers slipped inside the cotton briefs. I held my breath; her body strained with anticipation as I reached down. A moan escaped me as my fingers disappeared into the folds of her wetness. So soft. My fingers began their exploration, my passion fueled by the small shivers that already shook her body.

Gently at first, my fingers coaxed her, increasing in pressure, then pushing deeply inside of her. Slowly withdrawing to tease and stroke some more, then easing back inside. My fingers pressed deeply as my hand rubbed gently, coaxed, cajoled, urged.

She clasped me to her tightly, dragging her mouth from mine as she struggled to breathe. Her body stiffened, hovered, and squeezed against me tightly before falling back, shuddering, racked with tremors.

I held her, loving her. Wanting to say the words but not daring to.

The shivers in her body were quelled for a moment before she began to move against me again, the muscles inside her squeezing around my fingers, urging me deeper. I moved quickly this time, and she called out again, her body nearly lurching from the bed as she grabbed me and pulled me fully down on top of her, wrapping both arms and a leg around my body.

I let her hold me that way until her body stilled and her heartbeat quieted. Then I carefully lifted myself up until my face was above hers. I pressed my lips to her cheek, slowly moving to her temple, across her closed eyelids. My weight shifted to one elbow as I reached up and brushed damp curls from her forehead. She took deep breaths, trying to steady herself as a smile played on her lips. My lips caught hers again. Her response was automatic; lips parted to receive the kiss eagerly. I hovered there, feeling her lips search for mine, smiling as I felt her body stretch beneath me. At last her eyes opened, ever so slightly, shyly peeking from beneath her lashes.

"Good morning," I whispered.

She smiled lazily, face flushing. "Good morning," she replied, her voice low. "Do you always wake your lovers this way?"

Your lovers. I played the words in my mind again. *Lovers.*

"Only the very special ones," I told her, kissing her again. "Are you okay?"

Her eyes grew wide. "*Okay* doesn't even begin to describe how I feel right now. Try happy. Ecstatic. Surprised. And very, very amorous." She lifted a hand behind my head, planting a kiss on my mouth. "I thought you said last night that you wanted to go slowly. It makes me wonder just what you might call moving fast."

My face burned red and I dropped my eyes, self-conscious. "I couldn't help myself. I was holding you . . ." I stammered. "I'm sorry."

She put a finger to my lips. "Please don't say

that. I'm not sorry. Not at all. Please don't make me think that you regret this already."

"I don't." I jumped to assure her. "I'm not sorry, either. Just nervous," I admitted.

"That makes two of us." She smiled, and her hand went to my cheek, fingers brushing lightly against my skin. "You're a wonderful lover, Leslie." Her voice was low. "But I'm afraid that I won't know how to touch you . . ."

"You don't have to . . ."

"But I want to so much." She raised her head, mouth claiming mine yet again as she urged me back, rolling me over until she was on top of me, legs tangled in mine.

I reached down to tug at her shirt, pulling it over her head, reveling in the feel of her small naked breasts settling against mine. My hands fell to the small of her back, feeling the soft smoothness as she stretched above me. She continued to kiss me, one hand tangling in my hair as her mouth traveled to my throat and the other hand lightly caressing my shoulder.

I could sense the nervousness in her breathing and the heartbeat that thumped against me. Her touch was tentative as she lifted herself, trembling. She began to trace the curve of my breast. She was no longer kissing me, her eyes riveted on her own hand as it covered me, forcing a heavy sigh from my lips.

"Is this okay?" She lifted uncertain eyes to mine, and I was quick to reassure her, telling her that her touch was wonderful.

"You're so soft," she told me, voice full of wonder as she drew a hesitant finger across my nipple. My body reacted without volition. My quick intake of breath was sharp. She smiled down at me, eyes wide and dark as she grew more confident. She reveled in watching my reaction to her touch, and I closed my eyes to stifle my embarrassment. Both hands were on me now, beginning to explore in earnest as her lips followed. Her mouth was slow and wet. She trailed kisses down my neck and across my chest. Her tongue teased me as her mouth covered first one breast, then the other. Fingers and hands and mouth and tongue were everywhere, driving me wild, torturing me, pushing and pulling and forcing me to focus on nothing else. All the while, her voice came to me, whispering endearments, marveling at what she was feeling, amazed that she could bring me such pleasure.

She delighted in the shivers that coursed through my body, in the moans I could no longer contain. Each stroke was an unbearable mixture of torment and ecstasy, until finally she gave in. Her fingers hesitated only a bit before reaching down and finding me soaked with pleasure. In an instant, my body was racked with tremors as my arms crushed her against me.

Before I could catch my breath, she moved again, hands and mouth continuing to play along my skin. I reached out, exclaiming as I did, "Please." My hand found hers and I held it still. "I need a moment —" My body shivered involuntarily, and a laugh slipped from my mouth. My eyes finally opened to find hers wide with amazement. "You're killing me." I grinned, feeling too weak to hug her the way I wanted.

"Ooh, but what a way to go." She laughed

seductively, hugging me tightly and covering my face with kisses. Then she rolled away just enough to lean on one elbow, her head resting against the palm of her hand. She lifted the sheet and carefully tucked it around me before letting her fingers trail up and down my arm, soothing me.

I'd never seen such a look of pure pleasure on her face before. Her eyes sparkled with brilliance. A silly smile was plastered on her lips.

"You sure look awfully pleased with yourself," I laughed.

"I am." Her grin grew wider. "If I had known this would be so wonderful, I would have told you how I felt a long time ago."

"Really?" My heart had finally stopped racing. "And when might that have been, exactly."

She wrinkled her nose. "The truth?"

"Please."

"Well," she drew the word out slowly. "I already had suspicions the night you told me that you were gay." Her smile relaxed. "I was confused because I knew I was awfully fond of you. You just helped me put a name on it."

"That long ago?" I was shocked.

"Uh huh," she nodded. Her fingers were on my neck, brushing lightly, lingering over my collar bone. When she spoke again, her tone was low and full of regret. "It took me too long to admit how I felt. By the time I'd managed to let myself think about it, we weren't even speaking to each other."

She frowned, and I reached up and smoothed the crease between her brows. Then I brushed her hair from her down-turned face.

"So that's why you didn't seem to mind when I told you that Billy wanted us both down here," I said softly.

Her face colored guiltily. "I wanted the chance to be close to you again."

My fingers stroked her hair, comforting her. "And?"

"And then we went out that night with Billy and we met Michelle. That was a tough night for me," she admitted, sighing and moving her fingertips along my throat. "At first I was amused, watching you squirm when she came over to our table. But then I watched you dance with her, and something inside of me just snapped." She turned her eyes to mine, smiling wryly. "You were seducing each other right there in front of me. And all I could think of was that it should have been me out there instead of her."

"I don't believe it." I was dumbfounded, remembering how nervous and embarrassed I'd been when I had caught Sara watching us on the dance floor. "I had no idea at all. I thought you were probably disgusted by the whole thing. In fact, I thought that was why you went back to Boston the next morning."

She raised her eyes to the ceiling and sighed. "Not quite. I spent the whole night lying awake and arguing with myself about what I was feeling. You don't know how close I came to knocking on that door and spilling my guts to you right then. I got so scared about what I was feeling that I was packed and out of here before six the next morning."

I let my mind drift back, remembering the weekend. "But you were fine when you got back. In fact, that's when we really started spending time together again."

Sara nodded. "I spent that weekend convincing myself that I had confused my feelings. I had every intention of coming back and just being the best friend that I could possibly be. It worked for a while. But I was kidding myself." She bent down to kiss me again, slowly. "What about you?" she asked against my mouth.

"I think I've always had an itty-bitty crush on you." I lifted one hand, my thumb and forefinger about a half-inch apart to illustrate.

"I'm flattered," she teased.

"You didn't know?"

She shook her head. "No. You've always been careful to keep your distance from me." Her fingers found mine and they entwined automatically. "Would you ever have told me?"

My expression withdrew as I told her the truth. "No."

Her lips tugged down at one corner. "That rule again, huh?"

I nodded. "I never would have risked it," I said quietly.

She studied me for a while, her features softening. "Then I'm even more glad that I told you last night."

"Me too." I reached up to put both hands to her face, pulling her mouth down to mine in a long kiss. The stirring in my stomach began again. "Mmm. Should we order room service?"

"Coffee would be nice," she murmured in my ear as she lifted herself up and over until her full weight was on top of me.

I reached for the phone, blindly punching in the numbers and waiting for a response on the other end. Sara's tongue deftly circled my nipple as I ordered coffee and continental breakfast. She reached down, tugging my underwear past my knees as I dropped the phone back in its cradle. Her mouth found mine, suffocating me.

"How long will they be?" she asked breathlessly as my hand found her breast.

My mouth strained toward her. "Don't worry. We have plenty of time."

Chapter 14

Our joy continued through the weekend, spilling over into the week and flourishing throughout the month.

Each day brought a new level of intimacy, both physical and emotional. Physically, Sara was like a puppy with a new toy, delighting in every nuance of our bodies. She was eager to touch and be touched, to discover all of the hidden, special places that brought about such pleasure. She didn't hesitate to tell me whenever she discovered yet another way in which women and men were different. With wide-eyed looks of wonderment, she would slowly shake her head, amazed by one discovery after another. She would then smile a slow smile, wanting to tell me about it, coddling and cherishing each revelation before filing it away inside of her mind. While part of me cringed at such comparisons, I listened to every word, wanting to be there for her, wanting to make sure that I threw up no barriers between us.

Our lovemaking was gentle and exploring, heated and passionate. More than once I caught myself arrogantly setting out to prove that sexually, at least, there was nothing a man could give her that I couldn't. It was these times when I became most fiercely passionate, burying my fear and my anger in the passion that exploded between us. Guiltily, I was scared all the more by the intensity between us and the fear of it ending. I exhausted her with pleasure, knowing that for a time I had succeeded in my arrogance by the way she held me tightly, whispering how wonderful I felt.

Each day, the intensity seemed to increase. Until every look, every touch was charged with an unspoken, electrical current. All of it heightened, I'm sure, by the uncertainty. Everything was made new by the change in our relationship. And any time I found myself not quite believing what was happening, Sara would be near. Subtly pressing a knee against my thigh in the middle of a meeting. Placing her hands on my shoulders and leaning over me just a little too close as we poured over computer printouts spread out across my desk. Brushing my hand as she reached down to point out a particular problem.

Then there were the evenings. The weekends. Sara was alternately romantic and playful. Each day was an adventure, and I never knew quite what to expect.

It was on one of these nights as we lay quietly holding each other that she raised her head and smiled tenderly. "Tell me about kindergarten. What were you like? Who was your teacher? Do you remember much about it?"

"Whoa. Wait a minute. What's all this?" I tickled her lightly and chuckled.

The look she gave me was earnest. "I want to know everything about you. Who you are. Where you've been. Every important moment of your life." The eyes that held mine were clear and serious. I wondered if she knew how important those words were to me. How much it meant that she cared enough to want to know me.

"Mrs. Stembauch." I smiled, more at my thoughts of Sara than at the memory. "What about you?"

She shook her head. "You first. I'll tell you about me tomorrow night."

I liked the game. I looked up at the ceiling, letting the years fall away. I remembered being a little towheaded girl crying outside the school room, screaming at the top of my lungs, and refusing to let go of my mother's hand.

"I bawled like a baby the first day. I didn't want to leave my mommy."

"You poor thing." Sara looked so sad. "Tell me what happened."

So I told her, in vivid detail. And every night she'd ask where we left off. And every night one of us would tell the other of another moment or event from our pasts. Nothing was too insignificant as we spent hours talking and listening, prompting each other for explanations of feelings, going over each year of our lives in excruciating detail. And I came to know Sara. Not the Sara in the cool blue suit, but the little green-eyed imp with pigtails who always fought with her brother and teased her little sister mercilessly.

I had always known that I was attracted to Sara, and I could almost pinpoint when I knew that I wanted her. But it was during these late night conversations that I found myself adoring her, loving her, and falling for her completely.

"You are, without a doubt, the most attentive lover I have ever had." Sara whispered the words under her breath, so that only my ears could hear. It was a Thursday evening, and we had joined our coworkers at a local bar just after work. I had insisted that we join them, knowing that it had been some time since we had seen the group socially and that we still had a responsibility to keep up appearances. So there we sat, occasionally joining in the conversation, but remaining more a decorative fixture than a part of the group. We sat at one end of a large table while the others slung back their drinks.

I sneaked a look at her and saw that she was regarding me closely. Certain that no one could hear us, I asked her to elaborate.

A grin tugged at one corner of her mouth, but she remained pensive. "You're attentive in many ways, really. But right now I was thinking about the physical part."

I raised a glass of wine to my mouth to cover my smile. "Tell me," I said.

"You're so careful and sensitive. It's like you're listening to my body. Like you can hear what it's saying or screaming. And you know how to respond. Exactly how to touch me." She settled back in her chair and we surveyed the others. Her voice, when she continued, was quieter than before. "It's almost like I don't know where my body ends and yours begins, the way you hold me and kiss me and touch me in so many places at the same time. I feel overwhelmed and so full and rich inside."

Phew. My emotions swelled as my body reacted physically to her words. I took another sip of wine and gave her what I hoped was an inconspicuous glance. "I do all of that to you?"

She looked at me, studying my face. Her own features were a mixture of pain and wonderment and fear and lust. She nodded, her green eyes piercing mine, sending a shiver through my body.

Someone interrupted our conversation, planting himself in the chair beside Sara, chatting lightly. And suddenly I watched the professional Sara, the *straight* Sara, come smoothly to life. Smiling graciously. Laughing at just the right moment. My mind began to reel with déjà vu. Nothing was as it seemed. I was reminded, not for the first time and certainly not for the last, of the awkwardness of the situation. So tenuous.

Then beneath the table where no one could see, I

felt a stockinged toe seeking the top of my foot, stroking my ankle, and traveling up the calf of my leg. I joined in the conversation, smiling and laughing easily. The pressure of her knee against my thigh was a constant reassurance.

For nearly an hour we kept up the light social patter, all the while keeping up the pressure beneath the table. She continued to charm the others, periodically reaching over to squeeze my hand or tap my shoulder in what appeared to be a friendly, demonstrative way. But the looks she threw my way spoke of her longing and caused shivers to roll down my spine. I watched her, excited by the game we were playing, fascinated by the way she kept everyone hanging on every word. I watched her the way I had so often in the past, but knowing that for the present at least, she was mine. Knowing too, that the present may have to be enough. I told myself that the future didn't matter.

Finally, she turned to me, the carefully fixed smile on her lips as she asked if I was ready to go. "I'm getting tired and a little hungry," she explained. Then she took a gulp of her wine and leaned over, her voice barely above a whisper. "I want to swallow you up, and I want you inside of me when I do it."

The ache between my legs leaped to life, and I stifled my groan. Putty in her hands, I let her make excuses for us, going through the motions of wishing them well as we left.

We took our time making love that night. Stretching each moment. The sweetness excruciating. Afterward, we lay curled together, her head resting in the crook of my neck, her fingers tracing the outline of my body. She seemed pensive, and I waited for her to give voice to her thoughts as I knew she would.

"It's not easy, is it?"

"What's that?" I asked, dipping my fingers into the curls of her hair.

"Being gay."

I didn't respond right away, and she continued. "All I wanted to do at the bar back there was hold your hand. Such a simple thing. And I couldn't do it." She raised herself on one elbow until her face hovered above mine. "Do you ever get used to it?"

I felt the sadness in her words and could see it in her eyes. "You do. After a while," I told her. "It tends to make you appreciate the little things all the more."

"Don't you ever get angry about it?"

"Of course I do. I can get absolutely vehement about gay issues. But I've learned to temper my anger and choose my battles carefully." I sighed heavily, feeling inadequate, not knowing how to explain. "Sometimes I see things in the big picture. And sometimes I just have to take care of my own little world."

Sara nodded, carefully settling back into my arms. I could sense the questions that had begun in her mind. The same questions I had asked myself years ago. While I wanted to give her the answers, I knew that I couldn't try to persuade her to feel the way that I wanted. I could only hope that the answers, when they came, would lead her to me.

* * * * *

As much as I couldn't wait to tell Susan about the change in my relationship with Sara, I was reluctant to pick up the phone. I wasn't prepared to hear the disapproval that I was sure would come. Finally, it was Susan who called me on Sunday morning, just a week after Sara's confession.

We had just finished breakfast, and Sara had me pinned to the bed, teasing me and tickling me mercilessly. Sara had settled her full length on top of mine, kissing me slowly, when the phone began to ring. I was prepared to let it ring all day, but Sara raised herself up just enough to reach over and pick up the receiver.

"Hello?" She put the receiver to her ear, tipping it toward me just enough so that I could hear the voice on the other end.

"I'm looking for Leslie." I could hear Susan clearly, mouthing the name to Sara so that she knew who she was talking to. "Is this Michelle?"

Sara grimaced at the mention of Michelle's name, raising an eyebrow as she grinned impishly.

"Nope," she said. "Wrong girlfriend."

I stifled a laugh, hearing nothing but silence on the other end of the line. I could picture Susan in my mind, caught off guard and scrambling for something to say.

"Oh. I'm sorry," she recovered quickly. "This is Susan Richards. Is Leslie there?"

"Hi, Susan." Sara's voice caressed Susan's name. "She's right here. Just a second." She lowered the phone and dropped a loud kiss on my open mouth. "Shame on you for not telling her about us yet," she reprimanded me none too quietly. Then she grinned and lowered her voice. "I'm going to take a shower.

It'll give you two a chance to talk." She kissed me again and padded back to her room.

"Hello, Susan."

"Shame on you for not telling your best friend about the new woman," she mimicked Sara's words. "My god, Leslie. Do you have a revolving door to your room down there, or what?"

I chuckled, letting her play her game.

"What's going on?" she continued. "Who is she? What's her name?"

I braced myself for Susan's reaction. "Susan," I dropped my voice down, "it's Sara."

"Sara?" She was incredulous. "*The* Sara?"

"Uh huh."

"Ahh!" She screamed loudly in my ear. "I knew it. I knew it. I knew it. You dog. I told you." She spent the next minute or so congratulating herself on her accurate prediction.

"How did it happen? Tell me," she implored. "I can't believe it."

I hesitated, deciding not to go into the details. "She told me that she had feelings for me."

"Feelings? Uh-oh." I could hear the warning bells in her voice.

"I told her that I felt the same way."

"Yeah? Then what?" Susan continued to prompt me, barely giving me time to reply.

"We talked. We danced..." I let the sentence dangle, enjoying for a moment the way she was agonizing over my words. A mistake, I soon realized, because she was well ahead of me.

"Did you sleep with her?"

I cringed a little at her blatancy. Making love with Sara was so new, so precious, that it was impossible for me to be cavalier about it. My spine bristled, and Susan noted my silence.

"You did." I could hear the oohs in her voice. "When? Tell me."

"Every night, actually. Since last Friday."

"A week ago?"

"Uh huh."

"And you didn't call me?" Her voice was high.

"I'm sorry. It's still so new," I sighed and said quietly. "I've been on cloud nine, and I haven't wanted to break the spell."

She hesitated a bit. "This isn't like a one-night kind of thing?" Her voice had settled down, becoming pensive.

"No. It's like..." I struggled to find the right way to describe it. "It's like we're lovers now. We're together all the time."

Susan whistled long and low. Then there was silence on the other end of the line before she said, "You're happy with this."

I could hear the doubt in her voice, and I knew that she wanted to express caution.

"Very," was my quick reply.

"Leslie, I'm happy for you. But I have to tell you that I'm a little worried about this."

"Don't be."

"I don't want you to get hurt."

"Don't. Susan, please." My voice was emotional. "I don't want to think about that right now, okay?" Silence stretched on the other end. "I appreciate your concern. Really, I just want to enjoy this right now."

Susan's voice softened. "I suppose it's a little late for warnings, huh?"

"Yeah. I'm afraid it is."

The conversation went on for a short while longer. We changed the topic, and I explained that I probably wouldn't be back to Boston before Thanksgiving. Sara had to go there to see her folks, and I planned on flying back with her. I told Susan I'd keep in touch, and we ended the call.

I hesitated before getting out of bed. The phone call hung over my head like a threatening cloud. There were too many unanswered questions. But it was too soon to worry, I told myself. Anything could happen.

As much as I tried to insulate myself against my own fears, the outside world began to seep in. We were in my office, congratulating ourselves on another in a series of small successes when Sara was called away unexpectedly. Billy took the opportunity to pin me down.

"What's going on with you two?"

"What do you mean?" My smile didn't waver, my voice was nonchalant.

"Look," he began, his voice clipped. "I don't think anybody else has noticed. But it's obvious to me the way you two look at each other. I saw her touch you three times in the last fifteen minutes. A month ago she didn't even want to be in the same room with you."

I had expected Billy's teasing, but I was caught off guard by the anger in his tone. I looked at him evenly, trying to comprehend his hostility.

"Are you worried that the others will find out?" I asked.

"It wouldn't be cool, Leslie." He was scowling, and I became indignant.

My voice was cold. "Sara and I aren't going to do anything stupid. And you're not going to be outed any more than you already are."

He considered my words as he fingered the beard on his chin. "I know. I'm sorry. I shouldn't have said that."

Stubbornly, I refused to come to his rescue. I eyed him quietly, stung from the implications of his words. He sulked a little, then asked what had happened with Michelle.

"Nothing, really." I shrugged, not giving an inch. "Michelle is okay with this. We weren't serious about each other."

"Does that mean you and Sara are serious?" He raised a brow, his voice biting and doubtful.

I became uncomfortable and defensive, choosing my words carefully. "We haven't gotten that far yet." It was the truth. As close as we had become, we never spoke of the future. I let my mind dwell on this until Billy's harrumph interrupted my thoughts.

"Don't let her fuck with you, Leslie." His voice dropped down to a whisper. "Straight women and men are all alike. They fuck with you until they get bored, and then they go back to their own lives." The bitterness in his tone was clear. He had been hurt in the past, it was obvious. But hadn't we all? As much by a gay lover as by a straight one? A different kind of hurt, certainly, but a hurt all the same. As true as his words might have rung, I wasn't prepared to listen. Not yet.

My voice was cool when I replied. "I'm sorry if

that's been your experience, Billy. But I don't want to hear this right now."

His eyes glittered sardonically. "No, I'm sure you don't." He pushed himself from his chair and stood up, stretching briefly before strolling to the door. "But don't say I didn't warn you, doll," he called over his shoulder before disappearing around the corner.

Somehow I had managed for the most part to avoid my fears. Now, after only one brief conversation with Billy, fear was alive and thriving, swelling inside me, clutching at my heart and suffocating the life out of me.

Damn. Damn. Damn. Cursing, I turned in my chair to stare out of the window. Autumn had come to Atlanta. The trees were barren, reminding me that winter was just around the corner. Thanksgiving was only days away. The new year was fast approaching, and with it the conclusion of the project. We were scheduled to wrap everything up by the first week in January. I knew that, if anything, we'd beat the deadline, not go over it. I dreaded the thought, pushing it away, not wanting to think about what we would do, or how it would end.

"What's wrong with Billy?" I turned to find Sara sitting in the chair vacated by Billy a moment ago.

I looked at her. I choked on my words. I wanted to take her hand and run away, insulate us away from the world, away from anyone who might interfere.

"Why? What did he say to you?"

"He snarled at me when I ran into him down the hall."

I picked up a pencil and tapped the desktop, looking at her sadly and contemplating how to phrase my reply.

"Billy's figured out that there's something going on between you and me," I told her.

A frown creased her brow. "So? Why would that make him angry?"

I sighed and dropped the pencil, spreading my hands flat on top of the desk.

"It doesn't, really. I think he's projecting. You know," I waved a hand. "Equating you and me with something that he's been through before."

She continued to frown, then raised a brow as a sarcastic edge crept into her voice.

"Ah," she nodded. "I get it. The prevailing theme among you gay people."

I was offended by her choice of words. *You gay people*. "What's that supposed to mean?"

She kept her voice low. "Don't get involved with straight women and men. They'll only break your heart. Sound familiar?"

My face grew red, and I refused to reply, not liking the tone in her voice.

"Michelle alluded to it too. That night when I went to see her at the bar. In fact, it was the last thing she said to me when she hugged me good-bye." She looked sad.

"What did she say?" I prompted.

She looked at me, lips still pulled down in a frown. "She told me not to hurt you.'"

I cringed at the words. "I'm sorry. She shouldn't have said that."

Her features softened, and she brushed my

apology aside. "Don't apologize. Obviously, there's some significance if I keep hearing it from everyone."

Her expression was serious as she leaned forward, adjusting the jacket of her suit.

"I don't want to hurt you, Leslie." The words stung. Of all the ways she could have said it, she'd chosen those specific words. Not *I won't hurt you*, or *I'm not going to hurt you*. Those words might have calmed my fears. But no. She chose *I don't want to hurt you*.

She must have sensed the wound that was opening, because she stood, her eyes softening. "Come on. It's getting late. Let's go home."

The door to my hotel room had barely shut before her hands and mouth were on me. Lifting my skirt, cursing my nylon stockings, popping buttons as she pushed me back against the door. With her tongue in my mouth and hands on my breasts, I fought conflicting emotions. I was muddled in depression, wallowing in my fatalist attitude. Yet Sara was kissing and touching me with a fierceness that I hadn't experienced with her before.

"Don't do this," she was saying between kisses. "Don't shut me out. Don't give up, Leslie. Give it time. Give us time."

How well she knew me, saw through me. She claimed my body totally, and as I stiffened defensively, she began anew, with a ferocity I'd never known she possessed. My nylons were in shreds, and her fingers pushed inside me, shocking me with their roughness, their insistence. She held me against the door as my body stiffened, bringing me roughly to orgasm before my body relaxed. Then she was cooing in my ear, her gentleness now as overwhelming as the wildness before. My legs grew weak, and I fell against her, strong arms holding me close, not letting me fall. As the orgasm had ripped from me, so had the sobs. Tears fell uncontrollably, and she held me tight, soothing me, whispering to me. Then she moved me to the bed and undressed me, slipping her own clothes to the floor. She joined me on the bed, covering me with kisses, gently touching and caressing and coaxing me again. Making love to me again and again until at last sleep overtook us both.

Chapter 15

Time was beginning to spin away from us, and each day my sense of panic grew. I looked forward to the long Thanksgiving weekend with trepidation, knowing that Sara would be apart from me and with her family for most of the time. I worried about the outcome and what impact the old familiarity would have on her and on us.

We arrived in Boston early that Wednesday afternoon, stopping at her apartment in the North End just long enough for her to pick up an overcoat before making our way to Susan's house. After some initial awkwardness, I was surprised at the easy camaraderie that quickly emerged between Sara and Susan. Even as they teamed up to tease me mercilessly, my heart sang as I watched the two favorite women in my life test the limits with each other.

Sara and I spent the night there, curled up together on the little futon. In the morning, she gave me a long hug at the door and said that she'd miss me. "I'll call later. I'm sorry I don't know what my plans are for the rest of the weekend." She kissed me slowly, and I tried not to let her see my worry. She tilted her head back and tsked at me. "I really like Susan. Do you think I passed?"

I laughed. "I know you did."

She grimaced a little and kissed me again. "Have fun," she called and was gone.

As I'd expected, Susan couldn't say enough about her. "I'm really surprised by her," she told me as we sat across the kitchen table from each other, a mug of coffee in each of our hands.

"Why?" I grinned.

"I don't know," she shrugged. "She's gracious."

"Gracious?" What an odd term.

"Yeah. I can't think of a better word. Very nice. Charming. Gorgeous." Her voice was serious, surprising me, as she regarded me closely. "It's easy to see why you fell for her."

I beamed happily. "You don't blame me?"

"How could I?" I heard sincerity in her voice but saw something unspoken flicker across her face. I knew what she was thinking. My smile fell.

"Susan. I'm so scared." Tears sprung from out of nowhere.

"I know, honey." She reached over and wrapped a hand over mine. "Give it time."

"We're running out of time. The project's practically over." I sniffed and rubbed a sleeve across my face. "We haven't even talked about what we're going to do."

"Sooner or later you'll have to talk about it. But you can't let the worrying get in the way, Leslie. You have to trust her. As hard as that might be."

I knew that she was right, but it didn't quell my rising panic.

Susan's lover, Pam, had traveled to her family's home in Rhode Island for the day, so Susan and I went to her mother's house, as we had for the past four years. Feeling weary and stuffed, we returned home just after six o'clock to find Sara sitting on the front steps.

I was painfully aware of the haunted, faraway look in her eyes as I ushered her inside. Her teeth began chattering instantly, and I wrapped my arms around her, wondering just how long she had been sitting outside in the cold.

Susan lit a fire in the fireplace and busily set about making coffee as I tried my best to comfort Sara, steering her to the sofa and holding her loosely.

"I'm okay," she repeated the words several times under her breath as she gathered herself. Finally, with a steaming cup of coffee in her hands, her eyes touched Susan's briefly before focusing on mine. "I really am okay. I'm just a little shocked right now. And getting angrier and angrier every minute." She slipped a hand into mine, and I held it closely. Again she looked at Susan. "I don't know how you guys do it."

"Do what? What happened?" Susan leaned forward across the coffee table.

Sara inhaled deeply. "We were all sitting around the table having dinner when my sister started ribbing me, asking me when I was going to bring my new boyfriend home to meet the family. I asked her what made her think I had a new boyfriend, and my mother chimed in that I must have met somebody because I never come home on weekends anymore."

I stared at her numbly, able to guess at what must have happened, but unable to ask. Susan prompted her to continue.

"So," she shrugged, "I told them that I was seeing a woman."

Susan whistled long and low. I kept my eyes on Sara, cringing openly. I hadn't expected her to tell her family.

Anger crept into her voice. "The room went dead quiet like that." She snapped her fingers. "Then my little sister started giggling and telling me what a good joke it was. I sat there staring at each of them, and I started getting pissed. I told them that I wasn't kidding, that I was seeing a woman, and that we were happy. Then all hell broke loose."

"What did they say?"

"My sister started telling me how gross and disgusting I was. My obnoxious brother said 'Oh great, my sister's a fuckin' dyke.' My dad screamed at him to watch his mouth. Then everyone was screaming, and my mother just started crying."

"She started crying?"

Sara nodded. "Then she told me over and over that they'd help me get past it. She told me that maybe I should talk to our priest." Her voice grew high and loud as she became more animated. *"Our priest,* for godsakes. Nobody in that house has been to church in twenty years."

"Oh, Sara." My heart was aching for her.

"What happened next?" Susan asked.

"I told her that I didn't need a priest or a fucking shrink either. Then I left."

"You just left?" I asked, and she nodded.

"Wow." Susan was shaking her head, her brows knitted together.

"Are you okay?" I asked. "What are you going to do?"

Sara just shrugged. "I don't know. Nothing like that has ever happened to me before. My family never argues. I've always thought they were so cool."

Susan grunted. "Most families are rarely that cool. At least at first. You should have seen my family when I came out to them!" Susan spent the next hour telling Sara and me all of her coming out stories. I was thankful that she was there, taking control of the situation, helping to lighten the heaviness in the air.

Later that night, as Sara snuggled against me, I asked if she thought she should try to talk to her family again over the weekend, and she shook her head thoughtfully. "No. We all need some time to get used to the idea. They can reach me in Atlanta if they want to talk." She asked me then how my family had reacted when they'd found out about me, and I tried my best to explain.

"My brother hasn't talked to me in something like seven years. No great loss, really, because he was always a prick anyway. But I can't tell you that it still doesn't hurt sometimes." I paused for a moment. "The rest of my family are pretty cool, actually. But we certainly don't have the same relationship that we did." I became thoughtful. "I can understand why some of my friends decide not to tell their families at all."

She seemed appalled by this. "I can't imagine that. Don't their families catch on?"

"Probably. But most of them would rather just pretend they don't know. It's easier."

Sara looked so forlorn at my words that I reached out to squeeze her hand. "I can't help feeling responsible for all of this. I'm so sorry."

"It's not your fault, Leslie. It's not like you seduced me or anything." She eyed me carefully as a seductive smile touched her lips, causing my heart to turn over.

"I think it was the other way around," I smiled.

"God knows I tried," she smirked. "My mother would absolutely faint if she knew." The thought made her laugh, and then she quickly sobered. "I hope you can be patient with me, Leslie. I've got to think through everything right now, okay?"

We spent the rest of the weekend with Susan and Pam. Sara seemed to recover somewhat from the scene with her family, although I knew it weighed heavily on her mind. On Saturday night, the four of us ventured to Cambridge to go to a lesbian bar. We spent the evening drinking far too much and dancing nonstop. Sara completely enjoyed herself, and again I watched in fascination as she and Susan joked and laughed together easily. We stumbled out of the bar just after one A.M., a frigid blast of cold air greeting us. Sara slipped an arm through mine and snuggled close as we crossed a busy intersection to get to Susan's car. Susan and Pam walked a few steps ahead of us, holding hands and singing as we reached the car.

All at once, from out of nowhere, a dark sports car careened around the corner, nearly running us over as a carload of high school boys hung out the windows, screaming and hurling obscenities as they forced us to dive for the curb.

"Lezzies!"

"Fuckin' dykes!"

Tires screeching, they roared with cruel laughter as the car sped away.

"Bastards!" I heard Susan say.

Cheeks hot with humiliation, my eyes sought Sara's. She was sitting on the sidewalk, her legs pulled up, her arms across her knees. Her head was bent, resting on her forearms. I reached down and touched an arm.

"Are you okay?" I asked quietly, squatting in front of her.

She mumbled something unintelligible, and I covered her hands with my own. "What?" I asked softly.

"I said, I'm not a fucking dyke," she said evenly, her voice brittle.

My heart sank into my stomach.

She lifted her head and I could see tears of frustration welling in her eyes. "I don't want to be a *fucking dyke,*" she told me, her voice oddly cold and hollow.

We stared at each other as I remained frozen. Susan crouched down behind Sara, deftly placing a hand on either shoulder. My eyes flickered up to Susan's, and I knew instantly that she had heard Sara's declaration.

"They're assholes," Susan muttered, her fingers beginning to rub Sara's shoulders. "I'm sorry, Sara." Her voice was softly caressing. "I know it's been a tough weekend for you. But you can't let them get to you. That's what they want." She slipped her arms about Sara's neck from behind and gave her a quick hug. "And there's nothing wrong with what you and Leslie have."

I watched as Sara squeezed her eyelids against her tears and fell into the hug. "Why are you being so nice to me?" she asked of Susan.

"Because I like you, and Leslie loves you. That's enough for me." Her words were spoken matter-of-factly.

I cringed as Susan gave voice to the words I'd never said. Sara looked at me with dark, but clear eyes.

"I think you tell her more than you're telling me," she said quietly.

I stammered, not knowing what to say. Susan rescued me, standing up and reaching down to pull Sara to her feet. "She doesn't have to say anything. I know her like a book." She gave Sara a quick hug. "Come on. Let's get you home to a warm fire and a soft bed. Some quiet music. Maybe coffee..." Remarkably, Sara allowed Susan to tuck her carefully into the car, Pam and I falling in behind them.

* * * * *

Sara became withdrawn after that night. I could see and feel that she was trying hard not to show it. But her smile was tired, her eyes less bright, and her laughter forced. We stopped making love. Each night she curled into me like a frightened child. I held her close, trying to comfort and reassure her.

It was difficult for her to talk to me, but she tried, in little dribs and drabs. But her words were sketchy as she grew more and more lifeless.

Little more than a week after our return to Atlanta, she came to my office late in the afternoon. I looked up to find her in front of my desk, shuffling nervously from foot to foot. Her tongue did the dip and tuck thing several times in the span of a few moments. Warning bells went off in my head.

"What's wrong?" I asked, heart in my throat.

"We have to talk," she whispered. "Can you get away?"

I checked my watch. Nearly four o'clock. "Of course." I shrugged into a light overcoat and followed her outside. Shoulder to shoulder, we began the familiar walk back to the hotel. A sense of dread settled over me.

"What's going on?" I prompted her.

She took a deep breath, exhaling loudly. "I just finished talking with Dennis in Boston. Apparently we've picked up a new client, and he'd like me to fly out there and help them develop the specs."

My pace slowed as the words reached me. I tried desperately to remain calm. "Where's the company?" I asked, staring straight ahead, unable to look at her.

"Wisconsin."

Heart sinking, I clenched my jaw, trying to control my reaction.

"How soon?" My voice sounded strangled. "For how long?"

"Tomorrow. For as long as it takes." *Boom*. I stopped dead in my tracks, swinging around to face her.

"He can't do that." Desperately, my mind searched frantically for a way out. "We've got to do something. Maybe I can go with you." I searched her face, noting how pinched it looked. Her eyes reflected sadness.

"I can't believe this," I was saying. "Dennis wouldn't do this. I can't believe he didn't call me first to run it by me." I shook my head, then stopped, realization dawning.

"I called Dennis, Leslie. I told him things were just about wrapped up here and that there was no reason for both of us to stay. I asked him if there was another project he could switch me to."

My knees grew weak, and I felt like the wind had been knocked from my lungs. Sara reached out a hand to steady me. "I'm really sorry, Leslie. I panicked. I didn't know what else to do."

"You could have told me." I felt hurt, angry, and betrayed. "You could have told me that you wanted out."

"I don't want out. I want a chance to think. On my own. Without my family and without the safety of your arms every night. It's too easy to turn to you and expect you to make it all okay. You're too kind. Too understanding. I can see how much I'm hurting you, and I know you would let me do it indefinitely. I don't want to hurt you anymore."

"So you're going to run away." My tone was caustic.

She blinked hard at my words. "I don't think that's what I'm doing," she said quietly. "I'm fucked up, Leslie. I can't be a lesbian for you. If that's what I am, then it's something I have to be even when I'm not with you. I have to find that out."

I couldn't help the tears that began to well up and slip down my cheeks. Angrily, I bit my lip and looked away. "I know," I told her. "It's just so soon." My voice was cracking. "It just doesn't seem fair, you know?" I tried to smile at her through my tears but failed miserably. "I never got to tell you how I feel about you."

"And why not, Leslie?" she asked softly, knowing the answer.

"Too scared that I'd push you away," I admitted.

She nodded. "See? And I never talked about my feelings because I've been terrified by them. This isn't good for either one of us."

I blinked hard and wiped my eyes before studying her tired face. "I know that you're right. I just thought we'd have more time." I rocked back on my heels, feeling inadequate, feeling like a fool. *You knew better, kiddo,* I chided myself. "Will you call?"

She frowned as she watched me. "I already know that I will want to call you morning, noon, and night. But I can't. Not for a while. Not until I figure this thing out."

It was over. Pure and simple. *How had I ever let myself get involved with her?* It was over.

Chapter 16

We barely spoke the rest of the evening. I watched as one by one, all of her belongings were packed into one bag or another. Part of me wanted to run away. But instead I watched masochistically, unwilling to let go of her even a moment before I had to.

My throat burned from unshed tears as we held each other that night. But in the morning, when I woke to find the pillow beside me empty, I wept. A single sheet of hotel stationery greeted me, a brief message scrawled: *I do love you, Leslie. Sara.*

"Then why in the hell didn't you tell me?" I screamed at the empty room, the words wrenched from deep inside me. Curling up on that bed and holding her pillow in my arms, I cried as I had never cried before. I bawled and sobbed until I made myself sick to my stomach.

I made two phone calls. The first to Billy's phone mail, saying I had the flu and wouldn't be in for a few days. The second was to Susan. She was groggy with sleep as I squeaked out the two words. "She's gone."

Susan took charge. I reached out for my lifeline, and she was there. Before the afternoon was over, my rock had arrived at the door. Her arms went around me and my tears began to pour all over again.

I'm not quite certain how I got through the next few months. I spent the first few days locked in my hotel room with Susan, wallowing in self-pity, berating myself for having ever gotten involved with Sara. The little voice in my mind mocked me, saying *I told you so* over and over until I felt the chip settling on my shoulder and all the old defense mechanisms falling firmly into place. Susan recognized the signs, as she reluctantly returned to Boston.

The completion of the Atlanta project became my complete focus. I decided that I wanted to be back in Boston by Christmas, and I did everything necessary to meet the deadline.

During quieter, weaker moments, I allowed myself to believe that it wasn't really over with Sara. That she'd be back any day. I fantasized that she would show up on my doorstep on Christmas Eve, arms laden with gifts. I would laugh and tell her that she was the only gift I wanted.

But Christmas Eve came and went, as did Christmas day, and the day after that, without so much as a word from Sara.

I left Atlanta behind and returned to the Boston office after the holidays, anything but fresh and rested. Uncertain of my future, either personally or professionally, I wasn't prepared for the gossip that eagerly awaited me. I'd barely been settled for an hour when Amy, our departmental secretary, asked if I'd heard about Sara. The ringing in my ears began at the mention of her name. Through a fog, I heard that Kenny was in Wisconsin with her, and he reported that Sara was in bed, literally, with the owner of the client company. "And," she added in a hush as I struggled for air, "Kenny says he's a black man. Can you believe it?"

"Kenny is a racist pig," I replied evenly, dismissing her from my office. *Never get involved with a straight woman.* At least this bit of news was the push I needed, the permission that I needed to let go and move on.

As the end of January neared, I was thinking clearly and beginning to take charge of my life again. Susan and I scoured through the want ads every Sunday morning. We would curl up in front of the fireplace, reading through the advertisements, plotting and planning my new career.

It didn't take long to realize that finding a new job and, hopefully, a new career might take longer than I would like. I decided that it was time to confront Dennis with my frustration and let him know that I needed a new challenge. With this thought in mind, I wandered up the hallway to his office on Monday morning, stopping at Amy's desk just outside his door as she beckoned to me.

"Dennis said he wants to see you right away." Her eyes were wide with excitement as angry voices began to rise on the other side of the doorway.

"I can't believe you're doing this!" Kenny's voice boomed from inside the office, causing my skin to crawl.

"What's going on?" I turned back to Amy.

"Dennis just canned him. He made some kind of crack to Sara about her sleeping with that black guy, and she sent him packing." Her eyes grew wider with barely contained enthusiasm. "Can you believe it?"

Before I could reply, Kenny stormed from the office, eyes wild as he brushed past me and headed down the hall. Amy was instantly on her feet and chasing after him. I watched them and then took a deep breath. *Who needs this shit?*

I didn't want to go in that office. I didn't want to hear any more about Sara and the black man. *God. Didn't this guy have a name?* I walked across the tiled floor and peered inside to see Dennis hunkered down in his chair, leaning heavily across his desk. He seemed to be talking to himself, ranting and raving as I stepped inside to let him know I was there.

"You can't do that," he was saying. "I can't let you. You're too important to this company and to this project."

I stepped cautiously in front of him, watching as his eyes lifted to mine and a look of relief swept over him. "Leslie!" he called my name loudly, motioning me into the chair in front of the desk. He pointed to the speakerphone on his desk, and I realized he was talking to someone on the other end. "Talk to her, Leslie. She's threatening to quit. Tell her she can't do this to us."

I stared at him dumbly, slow on the uptake. "Who?"

"Sara." A cold sweat broke out on my brow as he turned back to the speaker. "Sara, Leslie's here with me."

Silence.

"Leslie?" Her voice sounded tired. My mind began to spin.

"Hi, Sara." I said the words flatly, unemotionally. My heart was pounding.

Again silence stretched. Dennis said, "She wants to quit, Leslie. Talk to her." He stared at me hard, causing me to shrink back into the chair. My tongue was tied as I stared back. Again the silence stretched too long.

"I've had enough, Dennis." Sara's voice came over the speaker again, filling the room.

"Look. I fired his ass. You don't have to deal with Kenny any more." He looked up at me, his eyes glaring into mine. "Tell her, Leslie."

I stared at him blankly. "I can't do that, Dennis." The look that he threw me didn't change my mind. "Sara knows what she needs to do. I'm not going to try convincing her otherwise." My voice was carefully quiet and controlled.

Dennis responded by reaching out and pressing a

finger to the mute button on the phone. "Get out," he hissed. "I'll talk to you later."

"I'm sorry, Dennis. She's burned out," I shrugged. *And so am I.*

He lifted his finger, looking tired as he folded his hands together. Resignation showed on his face. "Go keep an eye on Kenny," he told me. "Make sure he doesn't do anything stupid on his way out."

I nodded, then stood up and left the room.

" 'Bye, Les." Sara's words reached my ears just as I passed through the door to the hallway. I didn't turn back to reply.

When I arrived home that evening, Susan was lounging in the living room, an anxious frown on her face. The theme to the local evening news was playing on the television. I tossed my briefcase to the floor before falling in a heap beside her. "I don't think I can take it anymore," I said as I closed my eyes and leaned my head on her shoulder.

When she didn't reply after several seconds, I opened one eye and peered at her suspiciously. She wasn't usually so quiet. "What's up?" I asked.

"Sara called." I returned her steady stare and then, suddenly weary, slowly lifted myself from her shoulder. "She wants you to call her." I took the small piece of paper from Susan's outstretched hand and stared at the phone number scribbled there. I waited for my heart to race, but instead felt nothing.

"Did you talk to her?"

"Briefly."

I raised an eyebrow and she squirmed a little.

"She sounded uncomfortable, and I was probably a little bitchy."

A small smile touched my lips as I imagined the conversation. "I talked to her today," I whispered. "Well, actually, I think I said 'hi,' and that's about all." Briefly, I told her what had happened earlier.

We were quiet for a few moments while I looked at the phone number again. Why was I so reluctant? Why wasn't I racing to the phone? I shook my head and dropped the piece of paper to the coffee table.

"Are you going to call her?"

I squinted at Susan and shook my head. "I don't think so." She stared at me for a moment, then nodded, accepting my decision without question. She reached out and slipped an arm around my shoulders. I turned and lifted my legs to the table, snuggling into her arms as I turned my attention to the television. "How's Pam?" I asked.

"Shitty," she replied. "We never get along any more." I didn't bother contradicting her.

"Leslie?"

"Hm?"

"Have you ever thought that maybe you and I should be together?"

The meteorologist was standing in the middle of the United States. "Yeah," I admitted, "more than once."

I focused on the weather forecaster as he raved about the blizzard that was currently over the Midwest, and expected to dump up to two feet of snow in Wisconsin before continuing east. My mind drifted back to the snowstorm in Chicago, the memory of Sara laughing as a snowball splattered across my face. I remembered chasing her down the hall, wanting to kiss her even then.

My eyes dropped to the small white sheet of paper that teased me, daring me to pick it up. I sighed deeply and reached over to take Susan's hand.

Chapter 17

As promised, the Midwest was completely snowed under by morning. Local and national news agencies were predicting a similar fate for Boston before the day was over. Snow had already begun falling and was expected to continue all day. I toyed with the idea of not going to work at all. The traffic reports indicated that most commuters were doing just that, and I knew that most offices would be closing early. I compromised by pulling on a pair of worn-out jeans and an oversize sweater, thinking almost everyone would probably do the same.

I opted for public transportation that morning, shivering in the thick, heavy air that lay across the city. My attitude about work was beginning to scare me. It was so unlike me not to be excited about what I was doing.

Downtown Boston felt eerily like a ghost town. Perhaps I hadn't taken the storm warnings seriously enough. My office building was equally empty, so I puttered around in the computer room while coffee perked in the cafeteria. A full steaming cup finally in hand, I headed to my office and perched myself near the windowsill, wishing that I had brought Sara's phone number with me. My mind was clearer now, and I felt better prepared to talk to her. I knew why I was afraid to call. I was afraid to hear the rejection from her lips. Having her so far away had helped to dull the pain. It was easier simply to know it was over without ever hearing it said. I sat staring out the window, daydreaming about calling her, wishing I knew what to do about my career and my future, wondering if I could gather the courage to tell Dennis that I needed a break too.

By ten-thirty, just as the snow began piling up in earnest on the street below, I heard rumblings down the corridor. Dennis, no doubt. Nothing would keep that man from a day's work. I pulled myself together and decided to tell him I needed a change.

I walked down the hallway, stopping just outside Dennis's office and peeking around the corner. He was sitting at his desk, his back toward me. I leaned against the tiled wall, gathering my courage and going over in my mind what I would say to him.

More sounds down the hallway. Someone else had decided to brave the weather. Odd sounds, like someone tossing books into an empty box. The hair on my neck began to rise as I pushed myself away from the wall and padded down the hall toward the sounds. Sara's office. The noise was definitely coming from there. Maybe Kenny had come back and was up to no good. I pulled myself up with that thought in mind, ready to pounce if it were him. I sneaked around the open door and stood in the doorway.

It took a moment for her image to sink in. Sara was there, her narrow back toward me as she lifted books from the bookshelf on the far wall and dumped them without ceremony into an open box.

I placed a hand on the doorjamb to steady myself, my head and fingertips beginning to tingle as I became overwhelmed with anxiety. Her hair was longer, the curls made softer by its weight. It was loosely tied back with a single ribbon and reached all the way down between her shoulder blades. She was thinner than I'd remembered, her tight jeans easily two sizes smaller than my own. She wore a dark blue sweater, its sleeves pushed up over her forearms.

Mesmerized, I watched her clear two entire shelves before I found my voice.

"Hey." She jumped as the word left my lips, whirling quickly, instantly on the defense. I watched closely as recognition crossed her features, her face softening as a slow, tentative smile found her lips.

"Hi." The single word was like a caress, turning my knees to jelly.

"You look good." *What a stupid thing to say.*

"Thanks." She dropped the book she'd been holding and leaned against her desk, fingers playing absently with a pen. Her eyes roved quickly across my body. "You look tired."

Ouch. My smile was lame as I struggled for words. "What are you doing here?" I winced, knowing how cold my words sounded. "I mean, the storm. I thought you were stranded."

Sara practically shuddered. "As soon as I realized how bad it was going to be, I headed for the airport. I was going stir-crazy." She gave me an old knowing look. "You know how it gets..."

The image of me chasing her down the hallway of the hotel in Chicago swam in my mind. Then another image replaced it. Sara in a hotel room, in bed with a man. Too late, I realized by the frown that tugged between her brows that I was grimacing.

"Did Susan tell you I called?"

Sheepishly, I nodded.

"You didn't call back, did you?" She actually looked hurt. "I left a message and my flight number at the front desk for you."

I was incredulous. I suppose she had expected me to jump up as soon as she called and meet her at the airport. My chin lifted involuntarily as I shrugged. "I figured that waiting a few hours for me to call was nothing compared to the two months I waited to hear from you." It felt good to say the words, even though I regretted each one as they left my mouth.

Her lips were pursed together in a straight line.

"I suppose I deserve that." She looked defeated. "I'm sorry. I know I should have called you a long time ago."

"Oh? To tell me what? About the guy you're sleeping with?" My voice was quiet, mocking. "That's old news. It's all I've heard about for a month now." I was trying to hurt her, all the while praying she

205

would deny the accusations. She returned my stare steadily, without blinking. *Deny it! Deny it!* My heart sank. The rumors had been true after all.

"Kenny." She sounded resigned. She shook her head slowly, then met my gaze squarely. "This isn't quite going the way that I'd planned." She stepped over a box and made her way toward me. "We need to talk."

My back stiffened. I'd heard enough. Her lack of denial spoke volumes.

"Hey! You found her!" Dennis was standing behind me, bellowing over my shoulder before squeezing into the doorway beside me. "Did she tell you? I convinced her to take a leave of absence and think it over instead of resigning."

My eyes swept the room, taking in the boxes filled with Sara's personal belongings. Who did he think he was kidding? This didn't look like a temporary move to me. My eyes focused again on Sara, who was following me with her eyes and biting her tongue. Dennis was saying that he needed to talk to her, and I excused myself, backing out of the office and tearing my eyes away from hers.

After three steps, my temples began throbbing violently, and I rubbed them as I made my way down the hall to my office. Without a second thought, I grabbed my ski jacket and headed outside.

The snow plows were focused on the main streets downtown, and the sidewalks remained untouched. Snow clung to my ankles as I trudged up one street and then the next with no destination in mind. I was filled with anger and frustration. All the feelings I had carefully tucked away were flooding back.

Unresolved anger bubbled in my throat. Snow flakes whipped around me and tiny pellets of ice stung my face as I stumbled through the silent city.

The buildings along the wharf beckoned me until I found myself at ocean's edge, watching the whitecaps crash against the moorings. The wind whipped and swirled the snow into deep drifts and caused the bells on the tethered ships to clank in protest.

As I watched the ocean slapping against the docks, my thoughts returned to Sara. *It's over. Let it go. Just let it go.* I shivered and leaned over the railing just enough to watch the breakers directly below.

"I've been selfish." Sara's voice reached my ears over the howling wind. Without turning, I could feel her presence beside me. My jaw stayed carefully clamped shut.

"I know that you're angry. You have every right to be."

I didn't know how to reply, and I didn't trust myself to look at her.

"Say something, Leslie." She sounded frightened. "Yell at me. Please. Get it over with."

I looked out over the ocean, noting that the snow was too thick to see Logan Airport across the bay. I couldn't feel the anger anymore and I told her so. "It's all gone." I stole a brief glance at her, noting the way the wind whipped strands of hair across her face.

I knew she was watching me, expecting more. But I had nothing left to say. I shivered again and snuggled deeper into my coat.

"I need to explain," she began.

"No. You don't." I didn't want to hear the words. The excuses. The justification. But she didn't listen.

"I've been so caught up in myself, doing what I thought I had to do." Her words were stilted, halting. "I didn't even think about what this might be doing to you."

How could she be so unfeeling? Incredulous, I finally turned to face her. "You didn't think that it might hurt to hear that you're seeing some guy? Do you honestly think that being with you in Atlanta meant so little to me that I wouldn't care that you were with someone else now? Especially a man? Especially after the way you left?" I was insulted. "Did I really mean so little to you?"

Her eyes mirrored my pain. She bit back her words as she reached out to lay a hand on my arm. I tried not to flinch.

"Leslie. I didn't know what Kenny was saying to anyone back here." A gust of wind pushed her against me, and I automatically reached out to steady her. Her green eyes never left mine as she continued. "I assumed he was spreading rumors, but I wasn't certain. And I trusted that you would know better. I haven't been sleeping with anyone, Leslie. I swear."

Stunned, I watched her, uncertain that I could trust what she was telling me.

"I didn't leave Atlanta to find someone else. I left because my life had changed overnight and I wasn't prepared to handle the way people were reacting to that change. I didn't know if I could live that way." She swallowed hard and continued. "The mistake I made was thinking that I had to be away from you in order to find the answers. I was so afraid that what I was going through would come between us. I didn't want to blame you or hurt you anymore. And I could see how much it was hurting you." She shivered and leaned back against the railing. "I've been making plans and decisions and all kinds of assumptions. I had no business quitting my job or anything else until I'd talked to you."

I watched her, more confused than ever.

"Sara, I don't understand." I shook my head. "What do you want from me?"

She wrapped her arms around herself. The thin wool coat she was wearing couldn't possibly be warm. "Right now I want you to come home with me so we can talk without any more misunderstandings."

"You want to get snowed in with me and your roommate?" I smiled ironically.

She laughed. "She moved out last month. The place is practically empty."

I shook my head again and sighed, suddenly weary.

"What's the point, Sara? Trying to get over you has already taken so much out of me. I can't go through it again. It hurts too much."

"But that's exactly the point. I'm not over it. I never tried to get over it. I don't want to get over it."

"Sara. I'm telling you I can't do it. I can't wake up every day wondering whether or not you'll be around or wondering if I'm just filling in until you meet the right guy."

For the first time that morning, her eyes glittered with anger. She leaned closer, setting her jaw and lifting a finger that she pressed to my chest bone. I could feel the pressure even through the thick down jacket.

"You set me up to fail you from day one. You and all of your friends expected me to dump you. Expected me to go back to men. I gave you no reason to think that's what I was going to do." She dropped her hand, shoving it deep into the pocket of her coat as she continued her tirade, calmer now. "I've spent an awful lot of time going over this. I know that I've never felt closer to anyone else. I've never had a friend and a lover all wrapped up in one person before. I know that I could never have that with a man. And I'm certain that I never want another man to touch me. Not after making love with you. And I even know now that if you walked away from me right now, I'd still be a lesbian."

I stared at her, dumbfounded, remembering the words she had spoken that night outside the bar in Cambridge. *I'm not a dyke. I don't want to be a dyke.*

"Do you realize what you are saying?" I asked.

She tipped her head back and laughed, suddenly giddy. "Should I say it for you again?" she asked, her tone teasing. Then she faced me squarely and grinned broadly. "I'm a lesbian." She overenunciated the word proudly before lifting her voice to call out the words again at the top of her lungs. "I'm a lesbian!"

I was unable to stop the grin that found my lips. "I don't believe I'm hearing this."

"Believe it," she implored. "And please, stop punishing me because I never loved another woman before you." Her voice grew quiet.

Is that what I had done? Had I put a label on her and made assumptions based solely on that label?

I had. In that brief moment, the truth and wisdom of those words slapped harder and colder than the tiny pellets of ice that continued to pummel my cheeks.

"Weren't you straight at one time?" she was asking. "Before you fell in love with Julie and realized you were gay?"

I looked into her eyes and was overcome. "I never thought of it that way." I nodded grimly. "You're absolutely right," I admitted. The gusts of wind began to die down as thick, heavy flakes fell between us. "I'm sorry."

"I'm sorry, too. I've handled all of this so badly. But god, Leslie. If you have any feelings left for me, please don't push them away. Come home with me. Let's talk. We have so much to talk about." She reached for me again, her fingers curling around my arm.

I couldn't believe that after all the tricks my mind had played on me over the past months, she was actually here, talking to me this way. My resolve crumbled.

"You're right. We need to talk." I hesitated briefly, my mood lightening. "I don't suppose this means you're going to want to date me again."

She caught my unexpected smile and laughed a low, delicious laugh. "Date you?" She shook her head. "Nope. I want to marry you."

"Don't play with me, Sara." I stepped away from her.

She reached out both hands to grab my shoulders, her face contrite. "I'm not playing with you." Fear and doubt weighed heavily between us. "Oh, Leslie. Listen to me." She pulled me closer until her face was inches from mine. "I love you. Didn't you know that? I want to love you the way I wasn't able to before. Without holding back. Without either of us holding back."

I stared into her eyes, wanting to believe her, listening to the battle that raged between my heart and my head.

"Are you sure?" I croaked.

"I've never been more certain of anything in my life. The question is, what do you want, Leslie? How do you feel?"

I sighed, wondering if I could say the words, knowing that I had to. "I want a commitment. A real partnership."

She eyed me, a slow smile creeping to her lips. "A marriage of sorts?" she grinned.

Elation threatened to engulf me, and I carefully tempered it. "Of sorts," I agreed, feigning nonchalance.

Her grin grew and she nodded.

"And a house . . ." she dangled the sentence.

"In the suburbs. With lots of land," I finished.

She nodded again, enjoying the game. "With a puppy? Perhaps a kitten?"

"A puppy," I agreed. "And anything else that needs a home." My resolve was turning to mush.

"And what else, Leslie?" She reached out and in a single downward motion unzipped the jacket that covered me. Cold fingers reached beneath my sweater, tickling my belly before settling at my waist. "What else do you want?"

My knees were weak, and I sobered instantly. "I want you. I want us to be together." The words fell from my lips unchecked.

Her smile was full, lighting her eyes as her left

hand joined the right beneath my sweater. "And how do you feel about me, Leslie?"

I chuckled, finally realizing that she was fishing again, wanting to hear what I'd wanted for so long to tell her. "I love you, Sara." I reached out to brush her hair from her cheek, swallowing hard. "I've always loved you."

She smiled, leaning into me until her lips were brushing my neck. "At last," she sighed. "Tell me again."

I closed my eyes and let the moment wash over me as my arms reached out to hold her. "I love you, Sara."

I could feel her smiling. "I love you, Leslie." We held each other a moment longer before she lifted her head. "If we stay here long enough like this, maybe Dennis will see us and we won't have to worry about him trying to talk me out of leaving anymore." She kissed me quickly on the mouth and stepped back, slipping her arm through mine. "Come home with me?"

"I guess I don't have anything else to do," I shrugged, smiling.

We turned together to walk along the ocean's edge, listening to the silent beauty all around us as we trudged through the snow.

"I have a friend I want you to meet," Sara said as we tried our best to shelter our faces from the driving snow. I raised an eyebrow, uncertain where this was going.

"It's Tracy. I found her."

"No!"

"Uh huh. I called her folks and they gave me her

213

number. She forgave me, Leslie," her voice wavered just a bit.

"Sara, that's wonderful!" I hugged her tightly.

"I didn't ruin her life as I thought I had." Sara was elated, stumbling ahead of me playfully. "She met a woman right after high school, and they're still together. I told her all about you." The words were rushing from her lips.

I stopped for a moment, eyeing her carefully. "She helped you figure all of this out, didn't she. I mean about you. And me."

She stopped to face me, her smile wistful. "Yeah. She really did. Ironic, isn't it?"

I agreed that it was.

"I told her I was coming home to sweep you off your feet." She waited for me to catch up, slipping her arm through mine again when I'd reached her. "Am I doing okay so far?"

I dipped my head to one side. "Not bad. For a start. But you have an awful lot to make up for."

She laughed, squeezing my arm. "Ooh, I can't wait. I'm going to love every minute. Have I convinced you to marry me yet?" She ran off ahead of me again, bending to scoop up a handful of the wet flakes.

"Not yet." I played along. "But keep trying."

"I will, Leslie," she called. "I will."

My heart singing, I stopped and watched her begin to pack some snow together between the palms of her hands. *Uh oh.* Quickly, I bent to scoop up some snow, straightening just as the snowball splattered across my face. Gleeful laughter floated to my ears. When I opened my eyes I could see her far ahead now, sliding and slipping as she ran away from me, laughing and giggling at the top of her lungs. In a second I was chasing after her, my own laughter joining hers, knowing that this time when I caught her, I'd bury her in snow and cover her with kisses.

About the Author

Originally born and raised in Iowa, Linda now splits her time
between her home in Massachusetts and her new gal, Bella, in
Florida. While her biggest complaint remains that there simply
aren't enough hours in the day to do everything she'd like, she still
insists that she's the luckiest woman alive. Maggie continues to be
the sweetest thing that Linda has ever known.

Publications from
BELLA BOOKS, INC.
The best in contemporary lesbian fiction

P.O. Box 10543, Tallahassee, FL 32302
Phone: 800-729-4992
www.bellabooks.com

SUBSTITUTE FOR LOVE by Karin Kallmaker. One look and a deep kiss... Holly is hopelessly in lust. Can there be anything more?   ISBN 1-931513-62-7 $12.95

MAKING UP FOR LOST TIME by Karin Kallmaker. 240 pp. When three love-starved lesbians decide to make up for lost time, the recipe is romance. ISBN 1-931513-61-9 $12.95

NEVER SAY NEVER by Linda Hill. 224 pp. A classic love story... where rules aren't the only things broken.   ISBN 1-931513-67-8 $12.95

PAINTED MOON by Karin Kallmaker. 214 pp. A snowbound weekend in a cabin brings Jackie and Leah together... or does it tear them apart?   ISBN 1-931513-53-8 $12.95

THE WAY LIFE SHOULD BE by Diana Tremain Braund. 173 pp. With which woman will Jennifer find the true meaning of love?   ISBN 1-931513-66-X $12.95

GULF BREEZE by Gerri Hill. Could Carly really be the woman Pat has always been searching for?   ISBN 1-931513-97-X $12.95

THE TOMSTOWN INCIDENT by Penny Hayes. 184 pp. Caught between two worlds, Eloise must make a decision that will change her life forever. ISBN 1-931513-56-2 $12.95

BACK TO BASICS: A BUTCH/FEMME EROTIC JOURNEY edited by Therese Szymanski—from Bella After Dark. 324 pp.   ISBN 1-931513-35-X $12.95

SURVIVAL OF LOVE by Frankie J. Jones. 236 pp. What will Jody do when she falls in love with her best friend's daughter?   ISBN 1-931513-55-4 $12.95

DEATH BY DEATH by Claire McNab. 167 pp. 5th Denise Cleever Thriller.
                                          ISBN 1-931513-34-1 $12.95

CAUGHT IN THE NET by Jessica Thomas. 188 pp. A wickedly observant story of mystery, danger, and love in Provincetown.   ISBN 1-931513-54-6 $12.95

DREAMS FOUND by Lyn Denison. Australian Riley embarks on a journey to meet her birth mother . . . and gains not just a family, but the love of her life.   ISBN 1-931513-58-9 $12.95

A MOMENT'S INDISCRETION by Peggy J. Herring. 154 pp. Jackie is torn between her better judgment and the overwhelming attraction she feels for Valerie.
                                          ISBN 1-931513-59-7 $12.95

IN EVERY PORT by Karin Kallmaker. 224 pp. Jessica's sexy, adventuresome travels.
ISBN 1-931513-36-8 $12.95

TOUCHWOOD by Karin Kallmaker. 240 pp. Loving May/December romance.
ISBN 1-931513-37-6 $12.95

WATERMARK by Karin Kallmaker. 248 pp. One burning question . . . how to lead her
back to love? ISBN 1-931513-38-4 $12.95

EMBRACE IN MOTION by Karin Kallmaker. 240 pp. A whirlwind love affair.
ISBN 1-931513-39-2 $12.95

ONE DEGREE OF SEPARATION by Karin Kallmaker. 232 pp. Can an Iowa City librar-
ian find love and passion when a California girl surfs into the close-knit dyke capital of the
Midwest? ISBN 1-931513-30-9 $12.95

CRY HAVOC A Detective Franco Mystery by Baxter Clare. 240 pp. A dead hustler with a
headless rooster in his lap sends Lt. L.A. Franco headfirst against Mother Love.
ISBN 1-931513931-7 $12.95

DISTANT THUNDER by Peggy J. Herring. 294 pp. Bankrobbing drifter Cordy awakens
strange new feelings in Leo in this romantic tale set in the Old West.
ISBN 1-931513-28-7 $12.95

COP OUT by Claire McNab. 216 pp. 4th Detective Inspector
Carol Ashton Mystery. ISBN 1-931513-29-5 $12.95

BLOOD LINK by Claire McNab. 159 pp. 15th Detective Inspector Carol Ashton Mystery.
Is Carol unwittingly playing into a deadly plan? ISBN 1-931513-27-9 $12.95

TALK OF THE TOWN by Saxon Bennett. 239 pp. With enough beer, barbecue and B.S.,
anything is possible! ISBN 1-931513-18-X $12.95

MAYBE NEXT TIME by Karin Kallmaker. 256 pp. Sabrina Starling has it all: fame, money,
women—and pain. Nothing hurts like the one that got away. ISBN 1-931513-26-0 $12.95

WHEN GOOD GIRLS GO BAD: A Motor City Thriller by Therese Szymanski. 230 pp.
Brett, Randi, and Allie join forces to stop a serial killer. ISBN 1-931513-11-2 $12.95

A DAY TOO LONG: A Helen Black Mystery by Pat Welch. 328 pp. This time Helen's
fate is in her own hands. ISBN 1-931513-22-8 $12.95

THE RED LINE OF YARMALD by Diana Rivers. 256 pp. The Hadra's only hope lies in
a magical red line . . . climactic sequel to *Clouds of War*. ISBN 1-931513-23-6 $12.95

OUTSIDE THE FLOCK by Jackie Calhoun. 224 pp. Jo embraces her new love and life.
ISBN 1-931513-13-9 $12.95

LEGACY OF LOVE by Marianne K. Martin. 224 pp. Read the whole Sage Bristo story.
ISBN 1-931513-15-5 $12.95

STREET RULES: A Detective Franco Mystery by Baxter Clare. 304 pp. Gritty, fast-paced
mystery with compelling Detective L.A. Franco ISBN 1-931513-14-7 $12.95

RECOGNITION FACTOR: 4th Denise Cleever Thriller by Claire McNab. 176 pp.
Denise Cleever tracks a notorious terrorist to America. ISBN 1-931513-24-4 $12.95

NORA AND LIZ by Nancy Garden. 296 pp. Lesbian romance by the author of *Annie on
My Mind*. ISBN 1931513-20-1 $12.95

MIDAS TOUCH by Frankie J. Jones. 208 pp. Sandra had everything but love.
ISBN 1-931513-21-X $12.95